PUFFIN BOOKS

The Puffin Book of

Stories for Seven-Year-Olds

Wendy Cooling was educated in Norwich and, after a short time in the Civil Service, spent time travelling the world. On her return to England she trained as a teacher, went on to teach English in London comprehensive schools for many years and was for a time seconded as an advisor on libraries and book-related work in schools. She left teaching to work on the promotion of books and reading as Head of the Children's Book Foundation (now Booktrust), and later founded Bookstart, the national programme that helps to bring books to young readers. She continues to work with the programme as a consultant, as well as working as a freelance book consultant and reviewer.

The Puffin Book of Stories for

Seven-Year-Olds

Edited by Wendy Cooling

Illustrated by Steve Cox

PUFFIN

PUFFIN BOOKS

Published by the Penguin Group
Penguin Books Ltd, 80 Strand, London WC2R 0RL, England
Penguin Group (USA) Inc., 375 Hudson Street, New York, New York 10014, USA
Penguin Group (Canada), 90 Eglinton Avenue East, Suite 700, Toronto, Ontario, Canada M4P 2Y3
(a division of Pearson Penguin Canada Inc.)
Penguin Ireland, 25 St Stephen's Green, Dublin 2, Ireland (a division of Penguin Books Ltd)
Penguin Group (Australia), 250 Camberwell Road, Camberwell, Victoria 3124, Australia
(a division of Pearson Australia Group Pty Ltd)
Penguin Books India Pvt Ltd, 11 Community Centre, Panchsheel Park, New Delhi – 110 017, India
Penguin Group (NZ), 67 Apollo Drive, Mairangi Bay, Auckland 1310, New Zealand
(a division of Pearson New Zealand Ltd)
Penguin Books (South Africa) (Pty) Ltd, 24 Sturdee Avenue, Rosebank, Johannesburg 2196, South Africa

Penguin Books Ltd, Registered Offices: 80 Strand, London WC2R 0RL, England

penguin.com

First published 1996

047

This collection and introduction copyright © Wendy Cooling, 1996
Illustrations copyright © Steve Cox, 1996
All rights reserved

The moral right of the editor and illustrator has been asserted

The Acknowledgements on pages 163–5 constitute an extension of this copyright page

Set in 16/18pt Monotype Ehrhardt
Made and printed in England by Clays Ltd, St Ives plc

British Library Cataloguing in Publication Data
A CIP catalogue record for this book is available from the British Library

ISBN: 978–0–140–37460–5

www.greenpenguin.co.uk

Contents

Introduction

The stories in this book are stories to share and to talk about. By the age of seven most children are beginning to enjoy reading independently, but they will continue to appreciate the delight of listening to stories and sharing the reading experience. The stories here are wide-ranging – some quick to read and about real life, and some more complicated and set in other times or other lands – and they have all been enjoyed by seven-year-olds.

There is of course no such being as a typical seven-year-old and I hope these stories are as different as the readers. Encourage children to share the reading with you; to read some of the stories, such as "A Class Trip" and "The Wind That Wanted its Own Way" to you.

Talk about the stories, especially those that are unusual in style or language such as "The Old Man Who Wished He Coulda Cry" and "How the Camel Got his Hump". Tell your children other traditional stories as you read "Beauty and the Beast".

In reading, the talking about the book is almost as important as the story as it can fully involve children in quite difficult subjects and give an opportunity to discuss wider issues. Still, though, the most important aspect is enjoyment, as young children who find that reading is a pleasurable experience will want to move on to the next book and will more than likely develop quickly into real readers.

If your children particularly like some of the stories in this collection, look for more of the same kind or by the same author in your library or bookshop, and move on with your children to read more of Kipling's *Just So Stories*. Choose stories that both you and your children enjoy, and reading together will continue to be an important and pleasurable part of every day. Enjoy these stories!

Wendy Cooling

In the Middle of the Night

PHILIPPA PEARCE

In the middle of the night a fly woke Charlie. At first he lay listening, half-asleep, while it swooped about the room. Sometimes it was far; sometimes it was near – that was what had woken him; and occasionally it was very near indeed. It was very, very near when the buzzing stopped: the fly had alighted on his face. He jerked his head up; the fly buzzed off. Now he was really awake.

The fly buzzed wildly about the room, but it was thinking of Charlie all the time. It swooped nearer and nearer. Nearer . . .

Charlie pulled his head down under the bedclothes. All of him under the bedclothes, he was completely protected; but he could hear nothing except his heartbeats and his breathing. He was overwhelmed by the smell of warm bedding, warm pyjamas, warm himself. He was going to suffocate. So he rose suddenly up out of the bedclothes; and the fly was waiting for him. It dashed at him. He beat it with his hands. At the same time he appealed to his younger brother, Wilson, in the next bed: "Wilson, there's a fly!"

Wilson, unstirring, slept on.

Now Charlie and the fly were pitting their wits against each other: Charlie pouncing on the air where he thought the fly must be; the fly sliding under his guard towards his face. Again and again the fly reached Charlie; again and again, almost simultaneously, Charlie dislodged him. Once he hit the fly – or, at least, hit where the fly had been a second before, on the side of his head; the blow was so hard that his head sang with it afterwards.

Then suddenly the fight was over; no more buzzing. His blows – or rather, one of them – must have told.

He laid his head back on the pillow, thinking of going to sleep again. But he was also thinking of the fly, and now he noticed a tickling in the ear he turned to the pillow.

It must be – it *was* – the fly.

He rose in such a panic that the waking of Wilson really seemed to him a possible thing, and useful. He shook him repeatedly: "Wilson – Wilson, I tell you, there's a fly in my ear!"

Wilson groaned, turned over very slowly like a seal in water, and slept on.

The tickling in Charlie's ear continued. He could just imagine the fly struggling in some passageway too narrow for its wingspan. He longed to put his finger into his ear and rattle it round, like a stick in a rabbit-hole; but he was afraid of driving the fly deeper into his ear.

Wilson slept on.

Charlie stood in the middle of the bedroom floor, quivering and trying to think. He needed to see down his ear, or to get someone else to see down it. Wilson wouldn't do; perhaps Margaret would.

Margaret's room was next door. Charlie turned on the light as he entered: Margaret's bed was empty. He was startled, and then thought that she must have gone to the lavatory. But there was no light from there. He listened carefully: there was no sound from anywhere, except for the usual snuffling moans from the hall, where Floss slept and dreamt of dog-biscuits. The empty bed was mystifying; but Charlie had his ear to worry about. It sounded as if there were a pigeon inside it now.

Wilson asleep; Margaret vanished; that left Alison. But Alison was bossy, just because she was the eldest; and, anyway, she would probably only wake Mum. He might as well wake Mum himself.

Down the passage and through the door always left ajar. "Mum," he said. She

4

woke, or at least half-woke, at once: "Who is it? Who? Who? What's the matter? What? —"

"I've a fly in my ear."

"You can't have."

"It flew in."

She switched on the bedside light, and, as she did so, Dad plunged beneath the bed-clothes with an exclamation and lay still again.

Charlie knelt at his mother's side of the bed and she looked into his ear. "There's nothing."

"Something crackles."

"It's wax in your ear."

"It tickles."

"There's no fly there. Go back to bed and stop imagining things."

His father's arm came up from below the bedclothes. The hand waved about, settled on the bedside light and clicked it out. There was an upheaval of bedclothes and a comfortable grunt.

"Good-night," said Mum from the darkness. She was already allowing herself to sink back into sleep again.

5

"Good-night," Charlie said sadly. Then an idea occurred to him. He repeated his good-night loudly and added some coughing, to cover the fact that he was closing the bedroom door behind him – the door that Mum kept open so that she could listen for her children. They had outgrown all that kind of attention, except possibly for Wilson. Charlie had shut the door against Mum's hearing because he intended to slip downstairs for a drink of water – well, for a drink and perhaps a snack. That fly-business had woken him up and also weakened him: he needed something.

He crept downstairs, trusting to Floss's good sense not to make a row. He turned the foot of the staircase towards the kitchen, and there had not been the faintest whimper from her, far less a bark. He was passing the dog-basket when he had the most unnerving sensation of something being wrong there – something unusual, at least. He could not have said whether he had heard something or smelt something – he could certainly have seen nothing in the blackness: perhaps some extra sense warned him.

"Floss?" he whispered, and there was the usual little scrabble and snuffle. He held out his fingers low down for Floss to lick. As she did not do so at once, he moved them towards her, met some obstruction –

"Don't poke your fingers in my eye!" a voice said, very low-toned and cross. Charlie's first, confused thought was that Floss had spoken: the voice was familiar – but then a voice from Floss should *not* be familiar; it should be strangely new to him –

He took an uncertain little step towards the voice, tripped over the obstruction, which was quite wrong in shape and size to be Floss, and sat down. Two things now happened. Floss, apparently having climbed over the obstruction, reached his lap and began to lick his face. At the same time a human hand fumbled over his face, among the slappings of Floss's tongue, and settled over his mouth. "Don't make a row! Keep quiet!" said the voice. Charlie's mind cleared: he knew, although without understanding, that he was sitting on the floor in the dark with Floss on his knee and Margaret beside him.

Her hand came off his mouth.

"What are you doing here, anyway, Charlie?"

"I like that! What about you? There was a fly in my ear."

"Go on!"

"There was."

"Why does that make you come downstairs?"

"I wanted a drink of water."

"There's water in the bathroom."

"Well, I'm a bit hungry."

"If Mum catches you . . ."

"Look here," Charlie said, "you tell me what you're doing down here."

Margaret sighed. "Just sitting with Floss."

"You can't come down and just sit with Floss in the middle of the night."

"Yes, I can. I keep her company. Only at weekends, of course. No one seemed to realize what it was like for her when

8

those puppies went. She just couldn't get to sleep for loneliness."

"But the last puppy went weeks ago. You haven't been keeping Floss company every Saturday night since then."

"Why not?"

Charlie gave up. "I'm going to get my food and drink," he said. He went into the kitchen, followed by Margaret, followed by Floss.

They all had a quick drink of water. Then Charlie and Margaret looked into the larder: the remains of a joint; a very large quantity of mashed potato; most of a loaf; eggs; butter; cheese . . .

"I suppose it'll have to be just bread and butter and a bit of cheese," said Charlie. "Else Mum might notice."

"Something hot," said Margaret. "I'm cold from sitting in the hall comforting Floss. I need hot cocoa, I think." She poured some milk into a saucepan and put it on the hotplate. Then she began a search for the tin of cocoa. Charlie, standing by the cooker, was already absorbed in the making of a rough cheese sandwich.

milk in the pan began to steam.
...me, it rose in the saucepan, peered
over the top, and boiled over on to the hotplate, where it sizzled loudly. Margaret
rushed back and pulled the saucepan to
one side. "Well, really, Charlie! Now
there's that awful smell! It'll still be here in
the morning, too."

"Set the fan going," Charlie suggested.

The fan drew the smell from the cooker
up and away through a pipe to the outside.
It also made a loud roaring noise. Not
loud enough to reach their parents, who
slept on the other side of the house – that
was all that Charlie and Margaret thought
of.

Alison's bedroom, however, was im-
mediately above the kitchen. Charlie was
eating his bread and cheese, Margaret was
drinking her cocoa, when the kitchen door
opened and there stood Alison. Only Floss
was pleased to see her.

"Well!" she said.

Charlie muttered something about a fly
in his ear, but Margaret said nothing.
Alison had caught them red-handed. She

would call Mum downstairs, that was obvious. There would be an awful row.

Alison stood there. She liked commanding a situation.

Then, instead of taking a step backwards to call up the stairs to Mum, she took a step forward into the kitchen. "What are you having, anyway?" she asked. She glanced with scorn at Charlie's poor piece of bread and cheese and at Margaret's cocoa. She moved over to the larder, flung open the door, and looked searchingly inside. In such a way must Napoleon have viewed a battlefield before the victory.

Her gaze fell upon the bowl of mashed potato. "I shall make potato-cakes," said Alison.

They watched while she brought the mashed potato to the kitchen table. She switched on the oven, fetched her other ingredients, and began mixing.

"Mum'll notice if you take much of that potato," said Margaret.

But Alison thought big. "She may notice if some potato is missing," she agreed. "But if there's none at all, and if the bowl

11

it was in is washed and dried and stacked away with the others, then she's going to think she must have made a mistake. There just can never have been any mashed potato."

Alison rolled out her mixture and cut it into cakes; then she set the cakes on a baking-tin and put it in the oven.

Now she did the washing up. Throughout the time they were in the kitchen, Alison washed up and put away as she went along. She wanted no one's help. She was very methodical, and she did every-thing herself to be sure that nothing was left undone. In the morning there must be no trace left of the cooking in the middle of the night.

"And now," said Alison, "I think we should fetch Wilson."

The other two were aghast at the idea; but Alison was firm in her reasons. "It's better if we're all in this together, Wilson as well. Then, if the worst comes to the worst, it won't be just us three caught out, with Wilson hanging on to Mum's apron-strings, smiling innocence. We'll all be for it together; and Mum'll be softer with us if we've got Wilson."

They saw that, at once. But Margaret still objected: "Wilson will tell. He just always tells everything. He can't help it."

Alison said, "He always tells everything. Right: we'll give him something *to* tell, and then see if Mum believes him. We'll do an entertainment for him. Get an umbrella from the hall and Wilson's sou'wester and a blanket or a rug or something. Go on."

They would not obey Alison's orders until they had heard her plan; then they did. They fetched the umbrella and the hat, and lastly they fetched Wilson, still sound asleep, slung between the two of them in his eiderdown. They propped him in a chair at the kitchen table, where he still slept.

By now the potato-cakes were done. Alison took them out of the oven and set them on the table before Wilson. She buttered them, handing them in turn to Charlie and Margaret and helping herself. One was set aside to cool for Floss.

The smell of fresh-cooked, buttery

potato-cake woke Wilson, as was to be expected. First his nose sipped the air, then his eyes opened, his gaze settled on the potato-cakes.

"Like one?" Alison asked.

Wilson opened his mouth wide and Alison put a potato-cake inside, whole.

"They're paradise-cakes," Alison said.

"Potato-cakes?" said Wilson, recognizing the taste.

"No, paradise-cakes, Wilson," and then, stepping aside, she gave him a clear view of Charlie's and Margaret's entertainment, with the umbrella and the sou'wester hat and his eiderdown. "Look, Wilson, look."

Wilson watched with wide-open eyes, and into his wide-open mouth Alison put, one by one, the potato-cakes that were his share.

But, as they had foreseen, Wilson did not stay awake for very long. When there were no more potato-cakes, he yawned, drowsed, and suddenly was deeply asleep. Charlie and Margaret put him back into his eiderdown and took him upstairs to bed. They came down to return the umbrella and the sou'wester to their proper places, and to see Floss back into her basket. Alison, last out of the kitchen, made sure that everything was in its place.

The next morning Mum was down first. On Sunday she always cooked a proper breakfast for anyone there in time. Dad was always there in time; but this morning Mum was still looking for a bowl of mashed potato when he appeared.

"I can't think where it's gone," she said. "I can't think."

"I'll have the bacon and eggs without the potato," said Dad; and he did. While he ate, Mum went back to searching.

Wilson came down, and was sent upstairs again to put on a dressing-gown. On his return he said that Charlie was still asleep and there was no sound from the girls' rooms either. He said he thought they were tired out. He went on talking while he ate his breakfast. Dad was reading the paper and Mum had gone back to poking about in the larder for the bowl of mashed potato, but Wilson liked talking even if no one would listen. When Mum came out of the larder for a moment, still without her potato, Wilson was saying: ". . . and Charlie sat in an umbrella-boat on an eiderdown-sea, and Margaret pretended to be a sea-serpent, and Alison gave us paradise-cakes to eat. Floss had one too, but it was too hot for her. What are paradise-cakes? Dad, what's a paradise-cake?"

"Don't know," said Dad, reading.

"Mum, what's a paradise-cake?"

"Oh, Wilson, don't bother so when I'm looking for something . . . When did you eat this cake, anyway?"

"I told you. Charlie sat in his umbrella-boat on an eiderdown-sea and Margaret was a sea-serpent and Alison –"

"Wilson," said his mother, "you've been dreaming."

"No, really – really!" Wilson cried.

But his mother paid no further attention. "I give up," she said. "That mashed potato: it must have been last weekend . . ." She went out of the kitchen to call the others: "Charlie! Margaret! Alison!"

Wilson, in the kitchen, said to his father,

"I wasn't dreaming. And Charlie said there was a fly in his ear."

Dad had been quarter-listening; now he put down his paper. "What?"

"Charlie had a fly in his ear."

Dad stared at Wilson. "And what did you say that Alison fed you with?"

"Paradise-cakes. She'd just made them, I think, in the middle of the night."

"What were they like?"

"Lovely. Hot, with butter. Lovely."

"But were they – well, could they have had any mashed potato in them, for instance?"

In the hall Mum was finishing her calling: "Charlie! Margaret! Alison! I warn you now!"

"I don't know about that," Wilson said. "They were paradise-cakes. They tasted a bit like the potato-cakes Mum makes, but Alison said they weren't. She specially said they were paradise-cakes."

Dad nodded. "You've finished your breakfast. Go up and get dressed, and you can take this" – he took a coin from his pocket – "straight off to the sweet-shop. Go on."

Mum met Wilson at the kitchen door: "Where's he off to in such a hurry?"

"I gave him something to buy sweets with," said Dad. "I wanted a quiet breakfast. He talks too much."

Beauty and the Beast

RETOLD BY MICHAEL FOSS

In a far country, there was a merchant who had once been rich, but fell on hard times. His children, used to the best things, did not like their new life in a poor cottage. They had grown selfish and spoilt, and they complained bitterly. All except one.

She was the youngest, and she was neither selfish nor spoilt. In their little cottage she did the housework while the others complained. And because she was so willing and kind and pretty her father called her Beauty.

Then the merchant heard that a ship which he had thought was lost had now returned. Thinking that his fortune was saved, he prepared to go to the city and asked the children, just as he used to do, what presents he could bring them. The brothers and sisters wanted many expensive and foolish things, but Beauty asked for no present, except to see her father safe home.

"Oh, do accept something," her father said. And at last she asked for just one rose.

In the city, the arrival of the lost ship led to bitter arguments. The quarrel was taken to court, but after six months, while the lawyers grew rich, nothing was settled. In mid-winter, the merchant sadly set out for home, as poor as he had ever been. As he went, the snow was falling. In the gloom of the forest he could not find the path and the wolves howled. His horse stumbled, blinded by the weather.

In the night, the merchant almost gave up hope, for it seemed that death was coming to gather him. But next morning, suddenly he found himself in a strange land of sunlight. Instead of snow-covered forest paths, he saw an avenue of orange trees leading through gardens to a castle with towers that reached into the sky. He rode to the door and called, but there was no answer. He stabled his horse and entered the castle, going through rooms full of light and treasures and silence. In a far room he found food ready. Then, tired out by his journey, he slept.

When he awoke he was still alone. In the great, silent rooms he could find no one. He walked through the castle and through the gardens, seeing wonderful things on every side, and soon he began to think of his lost wealth and of his family. How happy they would be in this place! And since there seemed to be no one here, why should he not fetch them? Yes, he would do it. So he hurried to the stables, but as he passed through a pathway of roses he remembered his promise to his youngest, dearest child. He stopped and picked a single red rose.

At once, there was a terrible noise and a monstrous Beast stood in the path.

"Did I not," the frightful thing roared, "give you the freedom of my castle? How dare you steal my rose. I have a mind to kill you right now."

The merchant fell on his knees, begging for mercy. He explained his sad story, telling the Beast that the rose was for his daughter Beauty who was so good and kind. The Beast listened, grinding his ugly teeth. But when he spoke again, he was not quite so fierce.

"Your life will be saved," said the Beast, "if one of your daughters will offer to live with me here. Go now, and let them choose. Return at the end of the month. And do not think you can escape my power."

The horse seemed to know the way without any guide, but the merchant rode with a heavy heart. At the cottage, his children, who had feared that their father was dead, kissed him and laughed with joy. But when they heard what the Beast had said, they were angry and blamed Beauty for wanting the rose. Now they would have to fly to a far land, beyond the reach of the Beast.

But Beauty said: "Dear father, it is my fault. Come, let us go to the castle. I will stay with the Beast."

Sadly the merchant agreed, and sadly they returned to the strange castle, standing above the forest so shining and mysterious. They went through the rich, empty rooms and again found a meal made ready. When they were eating they heard a roaring of wind. The door burst open and the Beast came in like thunder.

"Well, Beauty," he bellowed, "have you chosen to stay?"

His looks were terrible to her eyes, but she answered quietly that she would stay.

"Very well, but your father must leave. He may take two trunks of jewels for his family, but he must never return. Choose what you like, than wave your father goodbye."

With many tears she kissed her father

goodbye. Then, worn out by sorrow, and by fear for the future, she fell on her bed and slept. She dreamed. She found herself in a golden country of meadows and woods. As she wandered there a handsome Prince appeared and spoke to her in a tender and loving way, begging her to be kind to him.

"Dear Prince," she sighed, "what can I do to help you?"

"Be grateful for what you are given," he replied, "but do not believe all you see. Above all, do not leave me. Rescue me from my cruel suffering."

Then the Prince faded away and his place in the dream was taken by a tall, lovely lady, who commanded Beauty: "Do not sigh for the past. Have faith and do not believe in appearances only. Great things await you in the future."

Thus began her life in the castle. Each day, she wandered through the rooms and the gardens. She met no one. Hidden hands prepared everything she might need. The days sped by with music and magical entertainments. And every evening, at supper, the Beast came, snorting and twisting his ugly great head.

"Well, Beauty," he roared, "are you going to marry me?"

But Beauty shook with fright and tried to creep away. And when the Beast had gone she went quickly to bed and entered the land of dreams where her Prince was waiting.

"Do not be so cruel," the Prince would beg, "I love you, but you are so stubborn. Help me out of my misery." He had a crown in his hands, which he offered her, kneeling and weeping at her feet.

But what did this dreaming mean? Beauty did not know. Her days were full of wonders. The sun shone always, and the birds sang. Bands of pretty apes were her servants. But each evening came the Beast, with his grim looks and his terrible question. And each night, in sleep, her Prince sighed for his freedom.

As the days passed, slowly she began to feel sorry for the Beast. He was kind, in his rough way, and gave her everything. Surely his ugliness was not his fault. But she was lonely too. She saw no one but the Beast. She missed her family. She began to sleep badly. Her dreams were full of worry. Her Prince seemed close to despair.

Then, one night, she dreamed that the Prince ran at the Beast with a dagger, meaning to kill him. Beauty stepped between them, pleading for the Beast, saying that the terrible monster was her friend and protector. The Prince disappeared and at once the tall lady was standing in his place.

"You will soon be happy," she told Beauty, "but only if you do not believe in appearances."

Next morning, waking tired and sad and lonely, she decided to ask the Beast for permission to see her family just once more.

When the Beast heard this he fell to the ground and groaned. But he said he could not deny anything to his Beauty. She could go, and take four chests of treasure with her. But if she did not return after two months, her Beast would die.

Her family were amazed to see her. Her father laughed and cried to have his favourite daughter back. And the four chests of treasure made even her brothers and sisters forget their troubles. They all begged her not to go back to the castle, and for a while she was so happy with her family that she never thought of the Beast.

Two months went by without her notice. Then, one night, she had another dream. She dreamed that she saw the Beast at the point of death. At once, she awoke. She remembered a ring that the Beast had given her, and turning it on her finger, she was carried in a flash to the castle. She ran through the great, silent rooms, but there was no sign of the monster. She dashed into the gardens and the park, calling his name, running here and there. At last, when night had fallen, she stumbled on his still body in the moonlight.

"Dear Beast," she cried, "are you dead? Oh, please forgive me. I never realized before that I love you. Now I fear I have killed you."

But his heart was still beating and her

presence began to revive him. In a while he was able to stagger to the castle. As he lay on a sofa, she heard him whisper in his sad, growling voice.

"Beauty, have you come back to me? Will you marry me now?"

And she answered at once: "Yes, dear Beast."

Then there was a blaze of lights, and loud music, and the Beast vanished. Instead, before her stood the Prince of her dreams, with the tall lady beside him. Beauty and the Prince took hands, and the lady smiled and blessed them.

"You have rescued my son," she told Beauty, "from the evil magic that has imprisoned him for so long in the hideous body of the Beast. When you chose him freely, you released the Prince from the spell. Now you will marry him. No longer will you be Beauty and the Beast, but the Prince and Princess of all this great and lovely land."

Back-to-Front Day

PAUL BIEGEL

Have you ever heard of Back-to-Front Day? It used to be celebrated once a year, you know, just like Twelfth Night and Easter; but Back-to-Front Day isn't celebrated any more and that is a great shame, because on Back-to-Front Day the grown-ups had to go to school.

And the children?

They were the masters and mistresses;

they were the policemen and bus conductors; they sat in the offices and telephoned to New York and Paris; they were firemen and drove through the streets with bells clanging; they were doctors and nurses and bakers and butchers and long-distance truck drivers.

"Stand in the corner, Mr Dryasdust!" said Marie. Marie was six and she had a class of twenty-three men and fifteen women. They were making much too much noise and not paying attention.

"Quiet!" cried Marie. "Mrs Oakapple, stop chattering. Mr Drumbody, sit up straight. Have you finished your sums yet?"

Granny was late for school. She got into bad trouble with Marie and as a punishment she was not allowed to draw.

Johnny was a policeman with his helmet balanced on his ears and his coat down to his knees and the bottoms of his trousers rolled up. He stalked down the street with huge strides and a stern expression on his face.

"Hm, hm, what does this mean?" he

cried sharply. "Why are you not at school?"

"Oh, Constable, I . . . I . . ." stammered the man, "I had to run an errand."

"Fiddlesticks!" said Johnny crossly. He took out his notebook and pencil. "Name?" he inquired.

"Mr Croop."

"Quite so," said Johnny. He wrote it down neatly, with two *o*s and then he blew his whistle and at once a police car with a blue flashing light appeared, driven by his friend Ernie.

"I have a truant here," said Constable Johnny. "Drive him straight to school."

Mr Croop was pushed into the car.

"You haven't heard the last of this," said Johnny.

He walked on and the next thing he saw was a brazen-faced woman coming out of a shop, as if she could do exactly as she pleased.

"Well, well, well, what's the meaning of this?" cried Johnny again.

"Not understand," said the woman. She was a foreigner, a tourist who didn't know anything about Back-to-Front Day.

"Oh," said Johnny. "Get along with you, then."

In the offices of the firm of Slosh and Splashing there was a tremendous bustle of activity.

Mandy was typing away on a typewriter with a red ribbon and Tommy was sitting behind the big desk which had at least four telephones on it, all ringing in turn.

"Hallo," said Tommy. "This is the director speaking . . . Yes, of course, twelve cases of paints. I'll get the driver to bring them along at once."

And he dialled a number of another telephone: "Hallo, Charlie, just take the truck and deliver twelve boxes of paints to Harry in the High Street."

At the hospital two small doctors climbed on one bedside chair together in order to look down Mrs Allsebest-Ramble's throat, and Nurse Janice stuck a plaster on Grandpa Johnson's leg.

But the best part of Back-to-Front Day was the evening because that was when the children put the grown-ups to bed. Very early. They told them a story, too – when the grown-ups had undressed obediently and cleaned their teeth and washed their hands.

"Don't forget your face, Daddy!" called Caroline.

Then the children went grandly down-stairs to watch television, or go to the pictures, or drop in on Johnny and Errol and Sandra.

Very, very late at night came the last television news bulletin, read by Arthur and Leonie.

"Good evening, boys and girls! Back-to-Front Day has been celebrated today throughout the country. A mother in Birmingham refused to go to school and was arrested by three seven-year-old policemen.

"In Westminster the Chancellor of the Exchequer got eight out of ten for arithmetic, but earned himself a detention for singing.

"A severe outbreak of fire in the New Forest was put out by Fireman Gary.

"Her Majesty the Queen did not return to Buckingham Palace until a quarter past five. Her teacher had had to keep her in for an hour after school.

"That was the news. Good-byeee!"

With the familiar notes of the National Anthem, Back-to-Front Day came to an end.

It's a pity we don't celebrate Back-to Front Day any more.

How the Camel Got his Hump

RUDYARD KIPLING

Now this is the next tale, and it tells how the Camel got his big hump.

In the beginning of years, when the world was so new-and-all, and the Animals were just beginning to work for Man, there was a Camel, and he lived in the middle of a Howling Desert because he did not want to work; and besides, he was a Howler himself. So he ate sticks and thorns and tamarisks and milkweed and prickles, most 'scruciating idle; and when anybody spoke to him he said "Humph!" Just "Humph!" and no more.

Presently the Horse came to him on Monday morning, with a saddle on his back and a bit in his mouth, and said, "Camel, Oh Camel, come out and trot like the rest of us."

"Humph!" said the Camel; and the Horse went away and told the Man.

Presently the Dog came to him, with a stick in his mouth, and said, "Camel, Oh Camel, come and fetch and carry like the rest of us."

"Humph!" said the Camel; and the Dog went away and told the Man.

Presently the Ox came to him, with the yoke on his neck, and said, "Camel, Oh Camel, come and plough like the rest of us."

"Humph!" said the Camel; and the Ox went away and told the Man.

At the end of the day the Man called the Horse and the Dog and the Ox together, and said, "Three, Oh Three, I'm very sorry for you (with the world so new-and-all); but that Humph-thing in the Desert can't work, or he would have been here by now, so I am going to leave him alone, and you must work double-time to make up for it."

That made the Three very angry (with the world so new-and-all), and they held a palaver, and an *indaba*, and a *punchayet*, and a powwow on the edge of the Desert; and the Camel came chewing milkweed *most* 'scruciating idle, and laughed at them. Then he said "Humph!" and went away again.

Presently there came along the Djinn in charge of All Deserts, rolling in a cloud of dust (Djinns always travel that way because it is Magic), and he stopped to palaver and powwow with the Three.

"Djinn of All Deserts," said the Horse, "*is* it right for any one to be idle, with the world so new-and-all?"

"Certainly not," said the Djinn.

"Well," said the Horse, "there's a thing in the middle of your Howling Desert (and he's a Howler himself) with a long neck and long legs, and he hasn't done a stroke of work since Monday morning. He won't trot."

"Whew!" said the Djinn, whistling, "that's my Camel, for all the gold in Arabia! What does he say about it?"

"He says 'Humph!'" said the Dog; "and he won't fetch and carry."

"Does he say anything else?"

"Only 'Humph!'; and he won't plough," said the Ox.

"Very good," said the Djinn. "I'll humph him if you will kindly wait a minute."

The Djinn rolled himself up in his dust-cloak, and took a bearing across the desert, and found the Camel most 'scruciatingly idle, looking at his own reflection in a pool of water.

"My long and bubbling friend," said the Djinn, "what's this I hear of your doing no work, with the world so new-and-all?"

"Humph!" said the Camel.

The Djinn sat down, with his chin in his hand, and began to think a Great Magic, while the Camel looked at his own reflection in the pool of water.

"You've given the Three extra work ever since Monday morning, all on account of your 'scruciating idleness," said the Djinn; and he went on thinking Magics, with his chin in his hand.

"Humph!" said the Camel.

"I shouldn't say that again if I were you," said the Djinn; "you might say it once too often. Bubbles, I want you to work."

And the Camel said "Humph!" again; but no sooner had he said it than he saw his back, that he was so proud of, puffing up and puffing up into a great big lolloping humph.

"Do you see that?" said the Djinn. "That's your very own humph that you've brought upon your very own self by not working. Today is Thursday, and you've done no work since Monday, when the work began. Now you are going to work."

"How can I," said the Camel, "with this humph on my back?"

"That's made a-purpose," said the Djinn, "all because you missed those three days. You will be able to work now for three days without eating, because you can live on your humph; and don't you ever say I never did anything for you. Come out of the Desert and go to the Three, and behave. Humph yourself!"

And the Camel humphed himself, humph and all, and went away to join the Three. And from that day to this the Camel always wears a humph (we call it a "hump" now, not to hurt his feelings); but he has never yet caught up with the three days that he missed at the beginning of the world, and he has never yet learned how to behave.

A Class Trip

MARGARET JOY

It was early on a hot summer's morning. Excited children from Miss Mee's class were already waiting to come into the playground at eight o'clock.

"I'll just unlock the gate," said Mr Loftus, jangling a bunch of keys. "I've never known children queue up for school before – what do you want to come to school so early for?"

41

"It's our trip day!" said Michael. "We're going to the seaside in a coach."

"Yes, with three on a seat, we can sit where we like, Miss Mee said," gasped out Jean, all in one breath. "And I've got a can of Coke and corned beef sarnies and a chocolate biscuit and –"

"That's nothing," boasted Gary. "I've got a yoghurt and a spoon and two chocolate biscuits and a bag of lamb 'n' mint sauce crisps and –"

Just then they all spotted Miss Mee walking across the playground with a haversack on her back. "Miss Mee. Miss Mee!" they shouted, and raced across to talk to her.

"What's in *your* bag, Miss Mee?" they asked.

"All sorts," said Miss Mee.

"Liquorice allsorts?" asked Mary.

"No, just all sorts of things," said Miss Mee. "You'll see."

After that, more and more people arrived and they waited in their classroom for the coach to pull up outside. While they waited, Miss Mee made sure they all had a picnic and money for an ice-cream, and then she made sure they'd all been to the toilet.

"Can we start our picnic now?" asked Nasreen. "I'm hungry."

"No," said Miss Mee. "Let your breakfast go down first."

At last the coach arrived and the driver sounded his horn: Berr-berr! The children cheered: "Hurray!" They gathered up their bags and went out to the coach.

The headmaster, Mr Gill, was there to see them off. "Have a lovely time," he said. "Drive carefully, Albert. And don't lose anyone, Miss Mee!"

Albert started the bus and the children waved goodbye to Mrs Hubb, the school secretary, in her office, and they knocked on the coach windows at Mr Loftus who was standing at the gate to see them off (and making sure that Albert didn't scratch the school's newly painted gateposts as he drove the coach through). Then, as the coach rolled down the hill, they all waved at their mums and grans and little brothers and sisters who were standing in the doorways to see them set off.

The coach was very, very hot, even though the roof was open and the breeze was blowing people's hair all over their faces. "Can we start our picnic now?" asked little Larry. "I'm hungry."

"No," said Miss Mee. "Let your breakfast go down a bit further first."

"My drink has spilt," said Nasreen. "I opened the top to make sure it was all there, and it spilt itself!"

Miss Mee opened her bag and took out a box of paper hankies. She helped to wipe the spilt orange juice off Nasreen's knees and off her shoes.

"My chocolate's melting," said Ian. "I was holding the bar in my hand so it wouldn't fall on the floor, and it's melting inside the silver paper!"

Miss Mee opened her bag again and took out an empty plastic bag. "Put it in here," she said to Ian. "Then it won't matter if it melts." Ian pushed the melting chocolate bar inside the clean plastic bag and put the bag inside his picnic box. He sucked the melted leftovers off his fingers.

"I feel sick," said Wendy.

"Come and sit with me at the front," said Miss Mee. "You can watch Albert driving."

"I can see the sea!" shouted Paul.

"*I* can see the sea," shouted Michael. "I saw it first."

"No you didn't," shouted Paul. "I saw it before you."

"Stop fighting, you two," said Miss Mee, "or I might leave you on the coach with Albert."

"Yeah! Watch it, you two!" said Albert over his shoulder. Michael and Paul decided to stop shouting at each other. They didn't want to miss going on the beach. The coach stopped in a car-park. Miss Mee counted all her children. Then everyone climbed out of the coach, clutching bags and buckets and spades.

"See you here at two o'clock," called Albert, and drove off.

They ran on to the sand and dumped their things. Then everyone wanted to paddle straight away. "Put your swimming things on if you've brought them," said

Miss Mee. "I'll help you if you can't manage yourselves."

"I've forgotten my swimsuit," moaned Brenda.

"Well, tuck your dress into your pants," said Miss Mee. That was easily done, and Brenda ran down to splash in the waves with the others.

"Ouch!" shouted Stevie. "A crab pinched my toes."

An extra big wave came up behind Imdad and knocked him on to his tummy in the water. "I'm surfing," he shouted. "Look, I'm surfing!"

Wendy trod on a bumpy pebble and sat down suddenly in the water. "Oh, Miss Mee, my pants are soaked," she howled. Miss Mee fished in her haversack.

"What a good thing I brought all sorts," she said. "Even spare pants!" She helped Wendy change her pants and laid out the wet ones to dry in the sun.

Sue ran along the beach screaming "Help! Help!" A little seaside donkey was trying to be friendly, following her to have its nose stroked. Sue wasn't used to donkeys. The donkey man came running up and caught the donkey by its reins. He showed Sue how to pat it and hold out a sugar lump on her flat hand.

"There you are," said the donkey man. "Prince only wanted to be friendly, you see." Sue cheered up then, and all the other children thought she was very lucky.

"Can we eat our picnic now?" asked Larry. "My breakfast's gone right down now."

"In half an hour," said Miss Mee.

Ian and Imdad started to make a sandcastle. It was a huge one, with pot-pie towers at each corner. Paul came and showed them how to make a moat all around the castle. Then the three boys raced to and fro to the waves, carrying bucketfuls of water to fill the moat. Then they dug a tunnel underneath the castle, scooping out the sand with their hands. It took ages to make, and just as they sat back on their heels to admire it, two large dogs came pelting across the beach and straight over the top of the castle. It was quite squashed. "I'm tired of castles," said Ian. "Let's dig a hole instead."

Mary went to the ice-cream van and bought a lolly. It was like a rocket, in stripes of red, yellow and orange. Mary ate half if it, but then it began to melt in the hot sunshine, and it fell off the stick into the sand. "Eughh!" said Mary. "I don't want a sandy lolly." So she buried the melting bits in a hole in the sand.

Asif bought a toffee apple. It was crunchy outside and soft inside, and very, very sticky. Asif got toffee round his mouth and on his nose and on his hair. After a while, he put the rest of his toffee apple on his lunch bag. "I'll just have a wash in the sea," he said. He ran off and knelt down in the water to splash his sticky face and hair. He ran back, dripping with water – just in time to see a seagull swooping low to snatch the rest of the toffee apple in his beak and fly off with it.

Barbara came limping up to Miss Mee. "I've cut my toe," she said. "There was a sharp shell and I trod on it."

Miss Mee looked in her bag and found a

tube of cream. "There," she said, "that'll make it more comfortable," and she gently rubbed it in.

"Picnic time!" she called next. Everyone cheered and raced up to where they had dumped all their belongings. They sat down and opened all the bags and packets and boxes that their mums had packed for them. Miss Mee had to open lots of cans of lemonade. Some of them had been shaken up in the coach and were too fizzy. They opened with a loud POP! and then swooshed over the top and on to Miss Mee's hands and dripped on to the sand. Miss Mee opened her bag and brought out a damp flannel to wipe herself with. "What a good thing I brought all sorts," she said.

Rosemary dropped one of her sandwiches on to the sand. "Eughh, my egg sandwich is all covered in sand," she said.

"You've got a sand sandwich," said Michael. "Ha, ha, ha!" and he laughed and laughed, and so did Paul and Gary and Pete.

"A sand sandwich," they laughed.

Rosemary was looking very upset, so her

twin, Barbara, said, "Here's a custard cream – have that instead." Rosemary cheered up then and ate the custard cream biscuit and took no notice of the boys.

Everyone was just finishing their picnic, when a little breeze started to blow. Dark clouds began to roll across the blue sky and the sun was hidden. It suddenly felt very cold and the breeze blew more and more strongly. Picnic bags began to rustle and dance away along the beach. Mouthfuls of food had gritty sand blown into them, packets of crisps rolled away. Drops of rain, huge and round as pennies, began to fall: splat! on to their picnic boxes, splat! on to the children's bare legs, splat! on to the dry, white sand.

"It's raining," shouted everyone. "There's going to be a storm."

"Oh, it's going to thunder," cried Wendy, and burst into tears.

"Rubbish!" said Miss Mee. "Of course it won't thunder. It never does on Fridays. – Now pack your bags quickly and pick up your bits and pieces. We'll go back to the car-park and wait for the coach."

She watched carefully while everyone packed their picnic papers and soggy towels, collections of seagull feathers and shells, wet bathing costumes, buckets and spades. They didn't leave a thing behind (except Mary's melted lolly and Rosemary's sand sandwich, and they were buried out of sight anyway).

By now the wind was blowing everyone along the beach, splattering them with rain. Sand was stinging their legs and arms. They all reached the car-park gasping for breath and covered in rain and sand. The car-park was quite empty. "Where shall we go?" asked the children, shivering and jigging up and down.

Berr-berr! came a sudden noise. They all turned their heads – and there was the coach. It slowly roared into the car-park, its headlights gleaming through the sheets of rain.

"Hurray!" shouted everyone. Albert stopped the coach and all the children piled in. Miss Mee counted them to make sure no one was missing. Then off drove Albert, back towards school.

"I can still see the sea," said Paul, looking out of the back window.

"No, you can't," said Michael.

"Quiet at the back there," growled Albert, and suddenly the coach was very quiet.

Then Albert switched on the coach radio. It was a pop music programme and most of the children began to sing the hits with the radio.

Miss Mee felt in her large bag and brought out a packet of black and white striped humbugs. "I forgot I had these," she said, and offered one to Albert and then to everyone else. The humbugs tasted of peppermint and were so big that they made people's cheeks bulge.

"I-ca-see-der-school," shouted Michael through his mouthful.

"No-you-cart," shouted Paul.

"Yes-I-ca."

"I-ca."

"I-ca."

"An-I-ca."

shouted everyone else, standing up to see.

Albert slowly stopped the coach in front

of the school door. It was still pouring with rain. The children had to jump over huge puddles before darting inside, their sandy hair dripping like water-rats' tails.

"Ah, *there* you are again!" said Mr Gill. "Well, you poor, wet, miserable, frozen creatures – what sort of a day have you had?"

"Oh, great!"

"It was a terrific day."

"The best trip we've ever had!"

"And how are you, Miss Mee? What sort of a day have *you* had?"

"Great," said Miss Mee. "And we've saved you a humbug."

The Old Man Who Wished He Coulda Cry

– A Caribbean British Story –

JOHN AGARD

Once there was a certain old man who wished he coulda cry.

The truth is he had forgotten how to cry.

He longed to hear the sniffing of his tears inside his pillow like when he was a small boy and couldn't get his own way.

All he heard these days was the sound of his footsteps creaking up the steps and the rats tumbling up the old newspapers and carrier bags that he never bothered to throw away.

For a moment the old man thought a cat would do for the rats. But that would mean buying more milk and even cat food, and he was the kind to peel a tangerine in his coat pocket so nobody would ask him for a piece.

But before the thought of a cat had gone out of his head, one sudden scratching started at his door.

From behind his curtain he could see a mannish-face cat standing with a look as if to say, "I ain't moving till you open this door."

Well, the old man certainly wasn't thinking of letting the cat in, but he just couldn't shut out that look on the cat face.

So he decided to let the cat in, and in no time the cat was diving among the old newspapers and scaring away the rats. Then the cat looked up at the old man as if to say, "What you going to do now?"

"Come on, here's a drop of milk for you, then out you go," was all the old man said.

But as he was putting the cat outside, his

blue eyes made four with the cat eyes, and he could swear he saw a teardrop slipping down the cat face.

When he was alone again, the old man thought this was a good moment to cry. Yet his eyes stayed dry as coconut, and as he sat there wishing for tears, suddenly dust started walking all over his bed.

He tried giving the coverlet a good shake-out. But this wasn't any ordinary dust.

This dust was walking over the wall-paper like fine ants, walking over the mirror, and even a photograph the old man had framed of himself in his soldier uniform when he was in the army.

He had to do something about this dust. But there wasn't a single thing his vacuum cleaner could do about it.

Just then he heard a voice calling at the door, "Leh me in. Leh me in. Fire chase me."

It was a strange voice and it belonged to the strangest broom the old man had ever seen. It had some bristles hard like corncob, some soft like cat fur.

Hear the broom. "Fire chase me. Leh me in." Hear the old man. "I'll let you in if you promise to work for me."

"I promise."

And in no time that runaway broom was swirling up the wall in a horsetail dance till the whole house was whistle bright! The old man couldn't believe he was seeing right. Mirror, bed, everything clean again!

But this wasn't a dream. And the broom standing there, asking for some milk, was as real as anything.

"Fancy that, a broom asking for milk!" the old man say, and he poured a little on a plate just to see what would happen.

To his surprise, the broom started to lap up the milk, and the next thing you know, the broom had changed back into the same cat that the old man had put outside.

"Tricky devil," the old man say. "You nearly did fool me, didn't you? But come on, out you go! Out!"

The old man pushed the cat out again, and when he went up to his room, he suddenly noticed something. Everywhere was free of dust except for one thing, and that was the photograph of himself in his soldier uniform. Dust was still walking like fine ants over the glass.

The old man looked at the photograph for a long time and wanted to cry. But no eye-water would come.

Then he found himself putting on his going-out shirt, which was unusual for him, because he hardly ever left the house. But he just had to find that cat.

The old man decided to walk down the road. He could see some young people dancing and drinking at the corner.

Suddenly he realized what day it was. August Monday. The long carnival weekend!

And here he was out on the street, looking for a strange cat, when he should be inside his house, away from all the crowds.

But it was too late. When he tried to turn back, he found a mass of people coming towards him. Black, white, brown, jumping up with a mad wave of hands, and the costumes giving back brightness to the summer day. The old man felt he'd never escape from this tangle of colour. The crowd was like a big strong wind sweeping him along.

And from the top of a truck, a band beating drums of steel sent a sweet deafness through the old man head. Even so he heard a voice behind him say:

> "Papa Doo-Doo
> Papa Doo-Doo
> Move yu foot
> Till yu feel like new."

The old man recognize that voice. It was the voice of the cat. But when he turned around, all he see was somebody, he couldn't tell if it was a man or a woman, dressed up in cat costume, and waving a long broom to the beat of the music.

> "Papa Doo-Doo
> Papa Doo-Doo
> Move yu foot
> Till yu feel like new."

The old man was sure – sure the voice was the same, but by now the cat-dancer had disappeared into the crowd.

59

Meantime, something was happening to the old man. See he moving to the music, yes, and in all that crowd of dancing black, white, brown, the old man could feel a wet trickle running down he cheek. And when he put up a hand, it wasn't sweat.

The old man couldn't believe he was crying small boy tears again. He couldn't remember the last day he feel so good.

The Farmer and the Snake

JULIUS LESTER

One cold winter morning a farmer was
walking down the road. He hadn't gone far
when he noticed a snake lying in the road.
He stopped and looked at the snake. It was
so cold that it couldn't move. The farmer
was a very kind-hearted man, and he felt
sorry for the snake. So he bent over and
picked it up. It was frozen so solid that it
was stiff and hard as a log. The farmer put

the snake inside his coat where it could get warm and thaw out. The farmer felt good about his kind act, and after a while he began to feel something moving around inside his coat. He peeked in. "Hallo there, Mr Snake. Are you getting warmed up?"

The snake didn't say anything.

Sometime later the snake wriggled harder. The farmer took another look at him. "You seem to be almost thawed out now."

"Almost," the snake said, flicking his forked tongue.

"Well, Mr Snake, I sure am happy. You would've frozen to death if I hadn't picked you up. Now I want you to promise me that you won't bite me when you get all thawed out. Remember, I did you a big favour."

The snake nodded. "I appreciate it, Mr Farmer. I really do. And you don't have to worry. I won't bite you."

"That's good."

Just as the farmer got close to town, the snake started moving around, and the farmer knew that he was all thawed out.

The farmer opened up his coat, and the snake crawled out and bit the farmer on the neck.

"Mr Snake!" the farmer cried. "You promised that you wouldn't bite me."

The snake looked at the farmer and said, "That's what I promised, Mr Farmer, but I'm a snake. You knew that when you picked me up. And you knew that snakes bite. It's a part of their nature."

Fortunately the farmer was close enough to town that he was able to get to the doctor and get some medicine before the snake's poison went to work on him. After that, though, the farmer knew. If it's in the nature of a thing to hurt you, it'll do just that, no matter how kind you are to it.

The Snowman

MABEL MARLOWE

A snowman once stood upon a hill, with his face towards the sunset. A very fine snowman he was, as tall as a soldier, and much fatter. He had two pieces of glass for eyes, and a stone for a nose, and a piece of black wood for a mouth, and in his hand he held a stout, knobbly club.

But he had no clothes at all, not even a hat, and the wind on the top of that hill was as bitter as wind could be.

"How cold I am! I am as cold as ice," said the snowman. "But that red sky looks warm." So he lifted his feet from the ground, and went tramp, tramp, tramping down the slope towards the setting sun.

Very soon he overtook a gypsy woman, who was wearing a bright red shawl. "Ha, that looks warm. I must have it," thought the snowman. So he went up to the gypsy woman and said, "Give me that red shawl."

"No, indeed! I cannot spare it on this wintry day," answered the gypsy. "I am cold enough as it is."

"Cold!" shouted the snowman in a very growlish voice. "Are you as cold as I am, I wonder! Are you cold inside as well as outside? Are you made of ice, through and through and through?"

"No, I suppose not," mumbled the gypsy, who was getting hot with fright.

"Then give me your red shawl this moment, or I shall strike you with my stout, knobbly club."

Then the gypsy took off her red shawl, grumbling all the time, and gave it to the snowman. He put it round his shoulders, without a word of thanks, and went tramp, tramp, tramping down the hill. And the shivering gypsy woman followed behind him.

Presently the snowman overtook a ploughboy who was wearing his grand-mother's long, red woollen mittens.

"Ha, they look warm! I must have them," thought the snowman. So he went up to the ploughboy and he said, "Give me those red woollen mittens."

"No, indeed!" said the ploughboy. "They belong to my grandmother. She lent them to me because my fingers were so cold."

"Cold!" shouted the snowman, in a very roarish voice. "Are your fingers as cold as mine, I wonder! Are your hands and arms frozen into ice, through and through and through?"

"No, I suppose not," mumbled the ploughboy.

"Then give me those red mittens, this

moment, or I shall strike you with my stout, knobbly club."

So the ploughboy drew off the warm mittens, grumbling all the time, and the snowman put them on, without a word of thanks. Then he went tramp, tramp, tramping down the hill. And the gypsy and the ploughboy followed him.

After a while he overtook a tame pirate, wearing a pirate's thick red cap, with a tassel dangling down his back.

"Ha! That looks warm! I must have it," said the snowman. So he went up to the tame pirate and he said, "Give me that red tassel cap."

"No, indeed!" said the pirate. "A nice cold in the head I should get if I did."

"Cold in the head!" shouted the snowman, in a very thunderish voice. "Is your head as cold as mine, I wonder! Are your brains made of snow, and your bones solid as ice, through and through and through?"

"No, I suppose not," muttered the tame pirate.

"Then give me that red tassel cap, this

moment, or I shall set upon you with my stout, knobbly club."

Now the pirate felt very sorry that he had turned tame, but he did not like the look of that knobbly stick, so he gave up his red tassel cap. The snowman put it on without a word of thanks. Then he went tramp, tramp, tramping down the hill, with the tassel bumping up and down. And the gypsy woman, and the ploughboy, and the tame pirate followed him.

At last he reached the bottom of the hill, where the village schoolhouse stood, and there was the village schoolmaster on the doorstep, looking at the sunset. He was smoking a glowing briar pipe, and on his feet were two red velvet slippers.

"Ha, those look warm! I must have them," said the snowman. So he went up to the schoolmaster and said, "Give me those red slippers."

"Certainly, if you want them," said the schoolmaster. "Take them by all means. It is far too cold today to be tramping about with bare toes," and he stooped and drew off his slippers, and there he stood in some bright red socks, thick and woolly and knitted by hand.

"Ha! Those look warm! Give them to me!" said the snowman.

"Certainly, if you want them," said the schoolmaster. "But you must come inside. I cannot take my socks off here, in the doorway. Come on to the mat."

So the snowman stepped inside the doorway, and stood upon the mat.

"Be sharp with those socks. My feet are as cold as solid ice," he grumbled.

"I am sorry to hear that," said the schoolmaster. "But I have a warm red blanket airing over the stove. Come in, sir. Sit on that chair by the fire, sir. Put your cold feet upon this snug red footstool, and let me wrap this red blanket around your legs."

So the snowman came into the schoolhouse, and sat upon a chair by the glowing fire, and put his feet upon the red footstool, and the schoolmaster wrapped the red blanket round and round his legs. (And all this while the gypsy woman, and the ploughboy, and the tame pirate were peering in at the window.)

"Are you feeling warmer?" asked the schoolmaster.

"No. I am as cold as an iceberg."

"Come closer to the fire."

So the schoolmaster pushed the chair closer to the fire, but the snowman gave him not one word of thanks.

"Are you feeling warmer now?"

"No. I am as cold as stone. My feet feel like icy water."

"Move closer to the fire," said the schoolmaster, and he pushed the chair right against the kerb. "There! Are you warmer now?"

"No, no, no! I cannot feel my legs at all. I cannot feel my back at all."

Then the schoolmaster pushed the chair quite close up against the stove. "Are you warmer now?" he said.

But there was no answer, except a slithery sliding sound, and the drip, drip, drip of black snow-water.

"Dear me!" whispered the snowman, in a gurgling kind of voice. "I have dropped my stout, knobbly club. My red slippers are floating into the ashpan. My mittens are swimming in a little river on the floor. My shawl is gone. My red tassel cap is slipping – slipping away. My head is going . . . going . . .''

Splosh! Splash! Gurgle!

"That's the end of him," said the schoolmaster, and he went to fetch the mop.

The gypsy woman, and the ploughboy and the tame pirate came in and picked up their things, and wrung them out, and dried them at the stove, and the schoolmaster put his red slippers on the hearth, and hung the red blanket over the back of the chair.

Then he picked up the stout, knobbly club and gave the fire a poke.

Small Gorilla and the Parsley

ANITA HEWITT

"Now eat up your carrot at once," scolded Mother Gorilla.

"Shan't! Don't want it!" said Small Gorilla. "Tired of carrot! Want parsley instead."

"Now please," his mother began to plead, but Father Gorilla frowned as he said: "If Small Gorilla is too fussy to eat his carrot, let him set out to find his own

72

parsley. In any case, it is time that he learnt to look after himself."

Small Gorilla threw down his carrot and scampered away.

"Parsley, fresh parsley!" he sang to himself, as he ran past the prickling thorn trees that grew near his home. "Oh fresh, Oh green, Oh juicy parsley!"

He looked in the tufty grass for parsley; he looked among the sweet potatoes; he searched here and he searched there, but not one leaf could he find.

"I'm hungry," he said. "Enormously hungry! Oh look! There's Baboon, and he's eating his dinner."

Baboon was eating a prickly pear.

"I suppose you wouldn't have seen any parsley," sighed Small Gorilla.

"Parsley!" said the Big Baboon. "What's parsley? *I* eat prickly pears for dinner. There, you can have one."

"Oh kind Baboon!" cried Small Gorilla. He took a big bite of the prickly pear, and squealed with pain as its sharp little spines scratched his mouth.

"Silly Gorilla!" Baboon scolded. "You

ought to have rubbed it hard on the ground." And he rubbed the prickly pear on the ground to scrape off the spines.

"I'll do that next time," said Small Gorilla, as he set off once more to look for his dinner. "Though I'd rather eat parsley, of course."

He looked among the rocks for parsley; he looked in the ditch beside the road; he searched here and he searched there, but not one leaf could he find.

"I'm hungry," he said. "Enormously, dreadfully hungry! Why, there's Secretary Bird, and he's eating his dinner."

Secretary Bird was eating a snake.

"I suppose you wouldn't have seen any parsley," sighed Small Gorilla.

"Parsley!" said Secretary Bird. "What's parsley? *I* eat snakes for my dinner. There, you can have one."

Small Gorilla remembered the prickly pear. He held the wriggling snake in his paw, and rubbed it hard on the ground. The snake darted its head upwards and bit Small Gorilla, right on his nose.

"Ee ee ee!" squealed Small Gorilla.

"Silly creature!" scolded Secretary Bird. "You ought to have jumped on the snake." He lifted his long thin legs off the ground, and thud! he jumped on the snake and killed it.

"I'll do that next time," said Small Gorilla, as he set off once more to look for his dinner. "Though I'd rather have parsley, of course."

He looked beneath the palm trees for parsley; he looked in the empty water-holes; he searched here and he searched there, but not one leaf could he find.

"I'm hungry," he said. "Enormously, dreadfully, terribly hungry! Oh, there's Hyena, eating his dinner."

Hyena was eating an ostrich egg.

"I suppose you wouldn't have seen any parsley," sighed Small Gorilla.

"Parsley!" said Hyena. "What's parsley? *I* eat ostrich eggs for my dinner. There, you can have one."

Small Gorilla remembered the snake. He lifted all four legs off the ground, and thud! he jumped on the ostrich egg, smashing into a sticky mess.

"Silly creature!" Hyena scolded. "You ought to have tapped the egg with a stone." He tapped an egg with a sharp little stone, and made a small hole.

"I'll do that next time," said Small Gorilla. "Though I'd rather eat parsley, of course."

He looked in the wet muddy ground for parsley; he looked beside the wide green river; he searched here and he searched there, but not one leaf could he find.

"I'm hungry," he said. "Enormously, dreadfully, terribly, horribly hungry. Ah! There's Chameleon eating his dinner."

Chameleon was catching gnats.

"I suppose you wouldn't have seen any parsley," sighed Small Gorilla.

"Parsley!" said the Chameleon. "What's parsley? *I* eat gnats for my dinner. There's one! It's flying over my head. You can have it."

Small Gorilla remembered the ostrich egg.

"But I can't tap that gnat with a stone," he said. "It won't keep still. I must throw the stone." He picked up a sharp little stone, and threw it, but the gnat flew away, and the stone hit Chameleon.

Chameleon danced and screamed with rage, and Small Gorilla fled in terror, pushing through the tangled grass and hurting himself on the prickly bushes. He ran and ran, gasping for breath, until he was aching and sore all over, and crying so much that he couldn't see where he was going.

"I'm hungry," he moaned. "I'm trembly with hunger."

But when he wiped away his tears, he thought at first that he must be dreaming. For there, quite close to him, were the prickling thorn trees that grew near his home.

"Home! I'm home!" breathed Small Gorilla. "I suppose there wouldn't be one little carrot; just one little carrot left over from dinner. Even a tough one would do."

But Small Gorilla was not to eat carrot that day for his dinner. For he heard, from behind the prickling thorn trees, the good sound of gentle chewing. He crept to the trees and peeped around them, then rubbed his eyes and stared and stared. For there, on the other side of the trees, grew fresh, green, juicy parsley. And among the parsley, eating their dinner, were Mother and Father Gorilla.

Small Gorilla walked slowly towards them, hanging his head. They smiled at him kindly.

"This is very good parsley," said Mother Gorilla.

"Juicy parsley!" said Father Gorilla.

"Oh, it *is*! It *is*!" laughed Small Gorilla. Then beside the prickling thorn trees there was no more talking. There was only the gentle chewing sound of a small, happy gorilla eating his dinner!

Horrid Henry's Holiday

FRANCESCA SIMON

Horrid Henry hated holidays.

Henry's idea of a super holiday was sitting on the sofa eating crisps and watching TV.

Unfortunately, his parents usually had other plans.

Once they took him to see some castles. But there were no castles. There were only piles of stones and broken walls.

"Never again," said Henry.

The next year he had to go to a lot of museums.

"Never again," said Mum and Dad.

Last year they went to the seaside.

"The sun is too hot," Henry whined.

"The water is too cold," Henry whinged.

"The food is yucky," Henry grumbled.

"The bed is lumpy," Henry moaned.

This year they decided to try something different.

"We're going camping in France," said Henry's parents.

"Hooray!" said Henry.

"You're happy, Henry?" said Mum. Henry had never been happy about any holiday plans before.

"Oh yes," said Henry. Finally, finally, they were doing something good.

Henry knew all about camping from Moody Margaret. Margaret had been camping with her family. They had stayed in a big tent with comfy beds, a fridge, a cooker, a loo, a shower, a heated swimming-pool, a disco, and a great big giant TV with fifty-seven channels.

"Oh boy!" said Horrid Henry.

"*Bonjour!*" said Perfect Peter.

The great day arrived at last. Horrid Henry, Perfect Peter, Mum and Dad boarded the ferry for France.

Henry and Peter had never been on a boat before.

Henry jumped on and off the seats.

Peter did a lovely drawing.

The boat went up and down and up and down.

Henry ran back and forth between the aisles.

Peter pasted stickers in his notebook.

The boat went up and down and up and down.

Henry sat on a revolving chair and spun round.

Peter played with his puppets.

The boat went up and down and up and down.

Then Henry and Peter ate a big greasy lunch of sausages and chips in the café.

The boat went up and down, and up and down, and up and down.

Henry began to feel queasy.

Peter began to feel queasy.

Henry's face went green.

Peter's face went green.

"I think I'm going to be sick," said Henry, and threw up all over Mum.

"I think I'm going to be –" said Peter, and threw up all over Dad.

"Oh no," said Mum.

"Never mind," said Dad. "I just know this will be our best holiday ever."

Finally, the boat arrived in France.

After driving and driving they reached the campsite.

It was even better than Henry's dreams. The tents were as big as houses. Henry heard the happy sound of TVs blaring, music playing, and children splashing and shrieking. The sun shone. The sky was blue.

"Wow, this looks great," said Henry.

But the car drove on.

"Stop!" said Henry. "You've gone too far."

"We're not staying in that awful place," said Dad.

They drove on.

"Here's our campsite," said Dad. "A *real* campsite!"

Henry stared at the bare rocky ground under the cloudy grey sky. There were three small tents flapping in the wind. There was a single tap. There were a few trees. There was nothing else.

"It's wonderful!" said Mum.

"It's wonderful!" said Peter.

"But where's the TV?" said Henry.

"No TV here, thank goodness," said Mum. "We've got books."

"But where are the beds?" said Henry.

"No beds here, thank goodness," said Dad. "We've got sleeping-bags."

"But where's the pool?" said Henry.

"No pool," said Dad. "*We'll* swim in the river."

"Where's the toilet?" said Peter.

Dad pointed at a distant cubicle. Three people stood waiting.

"All the way over there?" said Peter. "I'm not complaining," he added quickly.

Mum and Dad unpacked the car. Henry stood and scowled.

"Who wants to help put up the tent?" asked Mum.

"I do!" said Dad.

"I do!" said Peter.

Henry was horrified. "We have to put up our own tent?"

"Of course," said Mum.

"I don't like it here," said Henry. "I want to go camping in the other place."

"That's not camping," said Dad. "Those tents have beds in them. And loos. And showers. And fridges. And cookers, and TVs. Horrible." Dad shuddered.

"Horrible," said Peter.

"And we have such a lovely snug tent here," said Mum. "Nothing modern – just wooden pegs and poles."

"Well, I want to stay there," said Henry.

"We're staying here," said Dad.

"NO!" screamed Henry.

"YES!" screamed Dad.

I am sorry to say that Henry then had the longest, loudest, noisiest, shrillest, most horrible tantrum you can imagine.

Did you think that a horrid boy like

Henry would like nothing better than sleeping on hard rocky ground in a soggy sleeping-bag without a pillow?

You thought wrong.

Henry liked comfy beds.

Henry liked crisp sheets.

Henry liked hot baths.

Henry liked microwave dinners, TV, and noise.

He did not like cold showers, fresh air, and quiet.

Far off in the distance the sweet sound of loud music drifted towards them.

"Aren't you glad we're not staying in that awful noisy place?" said Dad.

"Oh yes," said Mum.

"Oh yes," said Perfect Peter.

Henry pretended he was a bulldozer come to knock down tents and squash campers.

"Henry, don't barge the tent!" yelled Dad.

Henry pretended he was a hungry *Tyrannosaurus Rex*.

"OW!" shrieked Peter.

"Henry, don't be horrid!" yelled Mum.

She looked up at the dark cloudy sky.

"It's going to rain," said Mum.

"Don't worry," said Dad. "It never rains when I'm camping."

"The boys and I will go and collect some more firewood," said Mum.

"I'm not moving," said Horrid Henry.

While Dad made a campfire, Henry played his boom-box as loud as he could, stomping in time to the terrible music of the Killer Boy Rats.

"Henry, turn that noise down this minute," said Dad.

Henry pretended not to hear.

"HENRY!" yelled Dad. "TURN THAT DOWN!"

Henry turned the volume down the teeniest fraction.

The terrible sounds of the Killer Boy Rats continued to boom over the quiet campsite.

Campers emerged from their tents and shook their fists. Dad switched off Henry's tape-player.

"Anything wrong, Dad?" asked Henry, in his sweetest voice.

"No," said Dad.

Mum and Peter returned carrying armfuls of firewood.

It started to drizzle.

"This is fun," said Mum, slapping a mosquito.

"Isn't it?" said Dad. He was heating up some tins of baked beans.

The drizzle turned into a downpour.

The wind blew.

The campfire hissed, and went out.

"Never mind," said Dad brightly. "We'll eat our baked beans cold."

Mum was snoring.

Dad was snoring.

Peter was snoring.

Henry tossed and turned. But whichever way he turned in his damp sleeping-bag, he seemed to be lying on sharp, pointy stones.

Above him, mosquitoes whined.

I'll never get to sleep, he thought, kicking Peter.

How am I going to bear this for fourteen days?

*

87

Around four o'clock on Day Five the family huddled inside the cold, damp, smelly tent listening to the howling wind and the pouring rain.

"Time for a walk!" said Dad.

"Great idea!" said Mum, sneezing. "I'll get the boots."

"Great idea!" said Peter, sneezing. "I'll get the macs."

"But it's pouring outside," said Henry.

"So?" said Dad. "What better time to go for a walk?"

"I'm not coming," said Horrid Henry.

"I am," said Perfect Peter. "I don't mind the rain."

Dad poked his head outside the tent.

"The rain has stopped," he said. "I'll remake the fire."

"I'm not coming," said Henry.

"We need more firewood," said Dad. "Henry can stay here and collect some. And make sure it's dry."

Henry poked his head outside the tent. The rain had stopped, but the sky was still cloudy. The fire spat.

I won't go, thought Henry. The forest

will be all muddy and wet.

He looked round to see if there was any wood closer to home.

That was when he saw the thick, dry wooden pegs holding up all the tents.

Henry looked to the left.

Henry looked to the right.

No one was around.

If I just take a few pegs from each tent, he thought, they'll never be missed.

When Mum and Dad came back, they were delighted.

"What a lovely roaring fire," said Mum.

"Clever you to find some dry wood," said Dad.

The wind blew.

Henry dreamed he was floating in a cold river, floating, floating, floating.

He woke up. He shook his head. He *was* floating. The tent was filled with cold muddy water.

Then the tent collapsed on top of them.

Henry, Peter, Mum and Dad stood outside in the rain and stared at the river of water gushing through their collapsed tent.

All round them soaking wet campers were staring at their collapsed tents.

Peter sneezed.

Mum sneezed.

Dad sneezed.

Henry coughed, choked, spluttered and sneezed.

"I don't understand it," said Dad. "This tent *never* collapses."

"What are we going to do?" said Mum.

"I know," said Henry. "I've got a very good idea."

Two hours later Mum, Dad, Henry and Peter were sitting on a sofa-bed inside a tent as big as a house, eating crisps and watching TV.

The sun was shining. The sky was blue.

"Now this is what I call a holiday!" said Henry.

Jimmy Takes Vanishing Lessons

WALTER R. BROOKS

The school bus picked up Jimmy Crandall every morning at the side road that led up to his aunt's house, and every afternoon it dropped him there again. And so twice a day, on the bus, he passed the entrance to the mysterious road.

It wasn't much of a road any more. It was choked with weeds and blackberry bushes, and the woods on both sides pressed in so closely that the branches met overhead, and it was dark and gloomy even on bright days. The bus driver once pointed it out.

"Folks that go in there after dark," he said, "well, they usually don't ever come out again. There's a haunted house about a quarter of a mile down the road." He paused. "But you ought to know about that, Jimmy. It was your grandfather's house."

Jimmy knew about it, and he knew that it now belonged to his Aunt Mary. But Jimmy's aunt would never talk to him about the house. She said the stories about it were silly nonsense and there were no such things as ghosts. If all the villagers weren't a lot of superstitious idiots, she would be able to rent the house, and then she would have enough money to buy Jimmy some decent clothes and take him to the movies.

Jimmy thought it was all very well that there were no such things as ghosts, but how about the people who had tried to live there? Aunt Mary had rented the house three times, but every family had moved out within a week. They said the things that went on there were just too queer. So nobody would live in it any more.

Jimmy thought about the house a lot. If he could only prove that there wasn't a ghost . . . And one Saturday when his aunt was in the village, Jimmy took the key to the haunted house from its hook on the kitchen door, and started out.

It had seemed like a fine idea when he had first thought of it – to find out for himself. Even in the silence and damp gloom of the old road it still seemed pretty good. Nothing to be scared of, he told himself. Ghosts aren't around in the daytime. But when he came out in the clearing and looked at those blank, dusty windows, he wasn't so sure.

"Oh, come on!" he told himself. And he squared his shoulders and waded through the long grass to the porch.

Then he stopped again. His feet did not seem to want to go up the steps. It took him nearly five minutes to persuade them to move. But when at last they did, they marched right up and across the porch to the front door, and Jimmy set his teeth hard and put the key in the keyhole. It turned with a squeak. He pushed the door open and went in.

That was probably the bravest thing that Jimmy had ever done. He was in a long dark hall with closed doors on both sides, and on the right the stairs went up. He had left the door open behind him, and the light from it showed him that, except for the hat-rack and table and chairs, the hall was empty. And then as he stood there, listening to the bumping of his heart, gradually the light faded, the hall grew darker and darker — as if something huge had come up on the porch behind him and stood there, blocking the doorway. He swung round quickly, but there was nothing there.

He drew a deep breath. It must have been just a cloud passing across the sun. But then the door, all of itself, began to swing shut. And before he could stop it, it closed with a bang. And it was then, as he was pulling frantically at the handle to get out, that Jimmy saw the ghost.

It behaved just as you would expect a ghost to behave. It was a tall, dim, white figure, and it came gliding slowly down the stairs towards him. Jimmy gave a yell, yanked the door open, and tore down the steps.

He didn't stop until he was well down the road. Then he had to get his breath. He sat down on a log. "Boy!" he said. "I've seen a ghost! Golly, was that awful!" Then after a minute, he thought, "What was so awful about it? He was trying to scare me, like that smart alec who was always jumping out from behind things. Pretty silly business for a grown-up ghost to be doing."

It always makes you mad when someone deliberately tries to scare you. And as Jimmy got over his fright, he began to get angry. And pretty soon he got up and started back. "I must get that key, anyway," he thought, for he had left it in the door.

This time he approached very quietly. He thought he'd just lock the door and go home. But as he tiptoed up the steps, he saw it was still open; and as he reached out cautiously for the key, he heard a faint sound. He drew back and peeked around the door jamb, and there was the ghost.

The ghost was going back upstairs, but he wasn't gliding now, he was doing a sort of dance, and every other step would bend double and shake with laughter. His thin cackle was the sound Jimmy had heard. Evidently he was enjoying the joke he had played. That made Jimmy madder than ever. He stuck his head further around the door jamb and yelled "Boo!" at the top of his lungs. The ghost gave a thin shriek and leaped two feet in the air, then collapsed on the stairs.

As soon as Jimmy saw he could scare the ghost even worse than the ghost could scare him, he wasn't afraid any more, and he came right into the hall. The ghost was hanging on to the banisters and panting. "Oh, my goodness!" he gasped. "Oh, my gracious! Boy, you can't *do* that to me!"

"I did it, didn't I?" said Jimmy. "Now we're even."

"Nothing of the kind," said the ghost crossly. "You seem pretty stupid, even for a boy. Ghosts are supposed to scare people. People aren't supposed to scare ghosts." He got up slowly and glided down and sat on the bottom step. "But look here, boy; this could be pretty serious for me if people got to know about it."

"You mean you don't want me to tell anybody about it?" Jimmy asked.

"Suppose we make a deal," the ghost said. "You keep still about this, and in return I'll – well, let's see; how would you like to know how to vanish?"

"Oh, that would be swell!" Jimmy exclaimed. "But – can you vanish?"

"Sure," said the ghost, and he did. All at once he just wasn't there. Jimmy was alone in the hall.

But his voice went right on. "It would be pretty handy, wouldn't it?" he said persuasively. "You could get into the movies free whenever you wanted to, and if your aunt called you to do something – when you were in the yard, say – well, she wouldn't be able to find you."

"I don't mind helping Aunt Mary," Jimmy said.

"H'm. High-minded, eh?" said the ghost. "Well, then —"

"I wish you'd please reappear," Jimmy interrupted. "It makes me feel funny to talk to somebody who isn't there."

"Sorry, I forgot," said the ghost, and there he was again, sitting on the bottom step. Jimmy could see the step, dimly, right through him. "Good trick, eh? Well, if you don't like vanishing, maybe I could teach you to seep through keyholes. Like this." He floated over to the door and went right through the keyhole, the way water goes down the drain. Then he came back the same way.

"That's useful, too," he said. "Getting into locked rooms and so on. You can go anywhere the wind can."

"No," said Jimmy. "There's only one thing you can do to get me to promise not to tell about scaring you. Go live somewhere else. There's Miller's, up the road. Nobody lives there any more."

"That old shack!" said the ghost, with a

nasty laugh. "Doors and windows half off, roof leaky – no thanks! What do you think it's like in a storm, windows banging, rain dripping on you – I guess not! Peace and quiet, that's really what a ghost wants out of life."

"Well, I don't think it's very fair," Jimmy said, "for you to live in a house that doesn't belong to you and keep my aunt from renting it."

"Pooh!" said the ghost. "I'm not stopping her from renting it. I don't take up any room, and it's not my fault if people get scared and leave."

"It certainly is!" Jimmy said angrily. "You don't play fair and I'm not going to make any bargain with you. I'm going to tell everybody how I scared you."

"Oh, you mustn't do that!" The ghost seemed quite disturbed and he vanished and reappeared rapidly several times. "If that got out, every ghost in the country would be in terrible trouble."

So they argued about it. The ghost said if Jimmy wanted money he could learn to vanish, then he could join a circus and get a big salary. Jimmy said he didn't want to be in a circus; he wanted to go to college and learn to be a doctor. He was very firm. And the ghost began to cry. "But this is my *home*, boy," he said. "Thirty years I've lived here and no trouble to anybody, and now you want to throw me out into the cold world! And for what? A little money! That's pretty heartless." And he sobbed, trying to make Jimmy feel cruel.

Jimmy didn't feel cruel at all, for the ghost had certainly driven plenty of other people out into the cold world. But he didn't really think it would do much good for him to tell anybody that he had scared the ghost. Nobody would believe him, and how could he prove it? So after a minute he said, "Well, all right. You teach me to vanish and I won't tell." They settled it that way.

Jimmy didn't say anything to his aunt about what he'd done. But every Saturday he went to the haunted house for his vanishing lesson. It is really quite easy when you know how, and in a couple of weeks he could flicker, and in six weeks the ghost gave him an examination and he got a B plus, which is very good for a human. So he thanked the ghost and shook hands with him and said, "Well, goodbye now. You'll hear from me."

"What do you mean by that?" said the ghost suspiciously. But Jimmy just laughed and ran off home.

That night at supper Jimmy's aunt said, "Well, what have you been doing today?"

"I've been learning to vanish."

His aunt smiled and said, "That must be fun."

"Honestly," said Jimmy. "The ghost up at grandfather's taught me."

"I don't think that's very funny," said his aunt. "And will you please not – why, where are you?" she demanded, for he had vanished.

"Here, Aunt Mary," he said, as he reappeared.

"Merciful heavens!" she exclaimed, and she pushed back her chair and rubbed her eyes hard. Then she looked at him again.

Well, it took a lot of explaining and he had to do it twice more before she could persuade her that he really could vanish. She was pretty upset. But at last she calmed down and they had a long talk. Jimmy kept his word and didn't tell her that he had scared the ghost, but he said he had a plan, and at last, though very reluctantly, she agreed to help him.

So the next day she went up to the old house and started to work. She opened the windows and swept and dusted and aired the bedding, and made as much noise as possible. This disturbed the ghost, and pretty soon he came floating into the room where she was sweeping. She was scared all right. She gave a yell and threw the broom at him. As the broom went right through him and he came nearer, waving his arms and groaning, she shrank back.

And Jimmy, who had been standing there invisible all the time, suddenly appeared and jumped at the ghost with a "Boo!" And the ghost fell over in a dead faint.

As soon as Jimmy's aunt saw that, she wasn't frightened any more. She found some smelling salts and held them under the ghost's nose, and when he came to she tried to help him into a chair. Of course she couldn't help him much because her hands went right through him. But at last he sat up and said reproachfully to Jimmy, "You broke your word!"

"I promised not to tell about scaring you," said the boy, "but I didn't promise not to scare you again."

And his aunt said, "You really are a ghost, aren't you? I thought you were just stories people made up. Well, excuse me, but I must get on with my work." And she began sweeping and banging around with her broom harder than ever.

The ghost put his hand to his head. "All this noise," he said. "Couldn't you work more quietly, ma'am?"

"Whose house is this anyway?" she demanded. "If you don't like it, why don't you move out?"

The ghost sneezed violently several times. "Excuse me," he said. "You're raising so much dust. Where's that boy?" he asked suddenly. For Jimmy had vanished again.

"I'm sure I don't know," she replied. "Probably getting ready to scare you again."

"You ought to have better control of him," said the ghost severely. "If he was my boy, I'd take a hairbrush to him."

"You have my permission," she said, and she reached right through the ghost and pulled the chair cushion out from under him and began banging the dust out of it. "What's more," she went on, as he got up and glided wearily to another chair, "Jimmy and I are going to sleep here nights from now on, and I don't think it would be very smart of you to try any tricks."

"Ha, ha," said the ghost nastily. "He who laughs last —"

"Ha, ha, yourself," said Jimmy's voice from close behind him. "And that's me, laughing last."

The ghost muttered and vanished.

Jimmy's aunt put cotton in her ears and slept that night in the best bedroom with the light lit. The ghost screamed for a while down in the cellar, but nothing happened, so he came upstairs. He thought he would appear to her as two glaring, fiery eyes, which was one of his best tricks, but first he wanted to be sure where Jimmy was. But he couldn't find him. He hunted all over the house, and though he was invisible himself, he got more and more nervous. He kept imagining that at any moment Jimmy might jump out at him from some dark corner and scare him into fits. Finally he got so jittery that he went back to the cellar and hid in the coal-bin all night.

The following days were just as bad for the ghost. Several times he tried to scare Jimmy's aunt while she was working, but she didn't scare worth a cent, and twice Jimmy managed to sneak up on him and appear suddenly with a loud yell, frightening him dreadfully. He was, I suppose, rather timid even for a ghost. He began to look quite haggard. He had several long arguments with Jimmy's aunt, in which he wept and appealed to her sympathy, but she was firm. If he wanted to live there he would have to pay rent, just like anybody else. There was the abandoned Miller farm two miles up the road. Why didn't he move there?

When the house was all in apple-pie order, Jimmy's aunt went down to the village to see a Mr and Mrs Whistler, who were living at the hotel because they couldn't find a house to move into. She told them about the old house, but they said, "No thank you. We've heard about that house. It's haunted. I'll bet," they said, "*you* wouldn't dare spend a night there."

She told them that she had spent the last week there, but they evidently didn't believe her. So she said, "You know my nephew, Jimmy. He's twelve years old. I am so sure that the house is not haunted that, if you want to rent it, I will let Jimmy stay there with you every night until you are sure everything is all right."

"Ha!" said Mr Whistler. "The boy won't do it. He's got more sense."

So they sent for Jimmy. "Why, I've spent the last week there," he said. "Sure. I'd just as soon."

But the Whistlers still refused.

So Jimmy's aunt went around and told a lot of the village people about their talk, and everybody made so much fun of the Whistlers for being afraid, when a twelve-year-old boy wasn't, that they were ashamed, and said they would rent it. So they moved in. Jimmy stayed there for a week, but he saw nothing of the ghost. And then one day one of the boys in his grade told him that somebody had seen a ghost up at the Miller farm. So Jimmy knew the ghost had taken his aunt's advice.

A day or two later he walked up to the Miller farm. There was no front door and he walked right in. There was some groaning and thumping upstairs, and then after a minute the ghost came floating down.

"Oh, it's you!" he said. "Goodness sakes, boy, can't you leave me in peace?"

Jimmy said he'd just come up to see how he was getting along.

"Getting along fine," said the ghost. "From my point of view it's a very desirable property. Peaceful. Quiet. Nobody playing silly tricks."

"Well," said Jimmy, "I won't bother you if you don't bother the Whistlers. But if you come back there —"

"Don't worry," said the ghost.

So with the rent money, Jimmy and his aunt had a much easier life. They went to the movies sometimes twice a week, and Jimmy had all new clothes, and on Thanksgiving, for the first time in his life, Jimmy had a turkey. Once a week he would go up to the Miller farm to see the ghost and they got to be very good friends. The ghost even came down to Thanksgiving dinner, though of course he couldn't eat much. He seemed to enjoy the warmth of the house and he was in very good humour. He taught Jimmy several more tricks. The best one was how to glare with fiery eyes, which was useful later on when Jimmy became a doctor and had to look down people's throats to see if their tonsils ought to come out. He was really a pretty good fellow as ghosts go, and Jimmy's aunt got quite fond of him herself. When the real winter weather began, she even used to worry about him a lot, because of course there was no heat in the Miller place and the doors and windows didn't amount to much and there was hardly any roof. The ghost tried to explain to her that heat and cold didn't bother ghosts at all.

"Maybe not," she said, "but just the same, it can't be very pleasant." And when he accepted their invitation for Christmas dinner she knitted some red woollen slippers, and he was so pleased that he broke down and cried. And that made Jimmy's aunt so happy, *she* broke down and cried.

Jimmy didn't cry, but he said, "Aunt Mary, don't you think it would be nice if the ghost came down and lived with us this winter?"

"I would feel very much better about him if he did," she said.

So he stayed with them that winter, and then he just stayed on, and it must have been a peaceful place for the last I heard he was still there.

The Princess in the Tower Block

FINBAR O'CONNOR

There was once a princess who was tired of being in fairy-tales. She was sick of getting locked up in towers by ugly witches and rescued by princes in ridiculous tights. She wanted to stay out after midnight without finding that her carriage had turned into a vegetable. And she had had enough of waking up every morning in a bed full of frogs claiming to be princes in disguise

110

(most of the princes she knew looked like frogs in disguise anyway).

So one morning, while the king and queen were watching the princes playing leap-frog (or the frogs playing leap-prince – it was sometimes hard to tell) the princess took her magic mirror and ran away to the big city. She moved into an apartment on top of the tallest tower block in town because she was used to living in tall places and thought that this was why people called her Your Highness.

Now, as you know, all fairy-tale princesses have long golden hair which they have to brush for hours every morning. But our princess was bored with that so she went to a hairdresser and had her head shaved. Then she put on an old pair of jeans, a T-shirt and a pair of trainers and stood before her magic mirror.

"Mirror mirror on the wall," she said. "Who's the coolest of them all?"

And the mirror replied:

"You're dressed in rags – you look a fright!
You must have stayed out past midnight.

*

The handsome prince will be appalled, he
Will not want a wife who's baldy!"

"Who cares?" said the princess and went
out on her balcony to look at the view.

"Coooeee!" called a distant voice. "Rapunzel, I'm home!"

Standing on the street far below, gaz-
ing adoringly up at her, was a prince in
bright-green tights.

"Oh, no," groaned the princess. "What
do you want?"

"Rapunzel! Are you up there, my beloved?" he cried. "Let down thy golden
locks that I might climb up and rescue
thee!"

"Clear off, you smarmy git!" shrieked
the princess.

The prince glared up at her.

"Loathsome hag!" he roared, shaking
his fist. "Release my beloved Rapunzel of
the golden hair or it'll be worse for you!"

"I'm not a loathsome hag," said the
princess crossly. "I'm a princess!"

"Forgive me, my beloved, I did not recognize thy baldy head," said the prince.

"But now that the witch has cut off thy golden tresses, how am I to scale yon lofty tower?"

"Do you have a ladder in your tights?" asked the princess sweetly.

"Well," replied the prince, "as a matter of fact I do."

"Then climb up that and see where it gets you!" she shrieked and stormed back indoors.

Just then the doorbell rang.

"Now what," sighed the princess as she answered it.

"Kissy kissy!" said a prince in yellow tights, taking her in his arms.

"Get off me, you slobbering oaf," cried the princess, struggling to escape.

"Wait a minute," said the prince as he let her go. "What are you doing up?"

"Why shouldn't I be up?" asked the princess.

"Because, Snow White," said the prince, "according to the seven dwarfs, your wicked stepmother gave you a poisoned apple that put you into an enchanted sleep.

I'm supposed to kiss you and wake you up!"

"The seven dwarfs?" cried the princess in horror. "Don't tell me they're here too!"

"They were too busy down the mine I'm afraid," said the prince, handing her a bag of smelly socks. "But they sent along some washing."

"I'll give them washing!" shrieked the princess furiously.

"Keep your voice down," hissed a prince in purple tights, popping his head in the door. "You'll wake the Sleeping Beauty!"

"She's awake already," said Prince Yellowtights.

"I'm not surprised," said Prince Purpletights. "With Cinderella's ugly sister here yelling her head off!"

"How dare you," said the princess. "I'll have you know I am nobody's ugly sister. I am a beautiful princess!"

"Well, you could have fooled me, baldy!" said Prince Purpletights rudely. "Anyway, if you're really a beautiful princess, why aren't you asleep?"

114

"Wait a minute," said Prince Yellow-tights. "Maybe she couldn't sleep because of the pea."

"Pee?" spluttered the princess. "What pee?"

"In the bed of course!" cried Prince Pur-pletights. "You can tell she's a real princess if a pea in the bed keeps her awake."

"I do not pee in my bed!" cried the princess indignantly.

But the princes were not listening. "Kissy kissy!" they slurped, reaching out for her.

"Unhand my darling Rapunzel, you swine!" cried Prince Greentights as he scrambled over the balcony.

"Where did you come from?" gasped the princess.

"Fellow called Honest Jack swapped me three magic beans for the Crown Jewels," replied the prince. "I just climbed up the beanstalk and here I am."

And indeed a gigantic beanstalk had sud-denly appeared outside, towering over the apartment block and vanishing into the clouds.

"Well," said Prince Purpletights doubtfully, "there are three of us and only one of her, so I suppose we'll just have to fight to the death."

"Oh . . . er . . . well . . . no, that's hardly necessary, is it?" stammered Prince Yellowtights. "I mean one of us might get hurt!"

"We could raffle her, I suppose," suggested Prince Greentights.

"I know," said Prince Purpletights, "Think of a number between one and ten and –"

"Now look here!" said the princess. "If you think –"

"What's that smell?" said Prince Greentights.

"What's that growling sound?" said Prince Yellowtights.

"What's that huge hairy thing coming in the door?" said Prince Purpletights.

"THE BEAST!" screamed all three princes and bolted for the balcony.

"GROOAR!" roared the Beast, charging after them. "You leave my Beauty alone!"

In a trice the three terrified princes were

scrambling down the beanstalk with the bellowing Beast in hot pursuit.

But as the princess rushed to the edge of the balcony to watch the chase, a voice even mightier than the Beast's thundered from somewhere in the clouds:

"FEE FO FUM, I'M COMING DOWN TO BITE YOUR BUM!"

"The Giant!" shrieked the three princes, and even the Beast looked worried.

"Don't worry," cried the princess, "there's a boy down there with an axe chopping down the beanstalk!"

"Jack!" screamed the three princes. "Don't do it, Jack!"

The Beast whimpered.

The Giant thundered.

The axe chopped.

The beanstalk swayed, creaked, cracked and fell.

Screams, howls, thuds, silence.

"Oh, dear!" said the princess, as she peered over the balcony.

Far, far below a giant was sitting in the middle of the street rubbing his head and looking puzzled.

Presently three very squashed-looking princes crawled from beneath his great fat bottom, carrying a groaning Beast between them.

"Come on, lads," said Prince Purple-tights. "Let's go back to the forest."

"But there are dragons there!" said Prince Greentights.

"And ogres," said Prince Yellowtights.

"And spiders," muttered the Beast, who didn't like creepy-crawlies.

"True," said Prince Purpletights. "But at least there aren't any princesses."

So the three princes, the Beast and the Giant returned to the forest and the princess stayed in her tower block. From time to time, her fairy godmother appeared to invite her to a ball, but the princess would not go. Occasionally, her wicked step-mother turned up with poisoned apples, but the princess never ate them. And once, she woke to find a frog sitting on her pillow blinking at her.

"If you kiss me," said the frog, "I'll turn into a handsome prince."

"If you don't go away," replied the princess, "I'll flush you down the loo!"

That was the last time she ever found a frog in her bed, and though she did marry somebody one day, he wasn't handsome, he wasn't a prince and he never, ever wore tights!

Kevin the Blue

CAROLINE PITCHER

Harry crept across the kitchen floor. His wellingtons squeaked like a finger rubbing a balloon and she heard him.

"Where do you think you're going, Harry Hodgkin?" she called.

"I'm going to see Kevin," he said and ran out of the back door.

"Who's Kevin?" she cried.

Harry kept on running, across the

garden, through the gate, down the hillside speckled with cowslips to the stream.

"She can stay with that baby," he muttered. "I'm going to see Kevin the Blue. He isn't sick on me, he doesn't dribble and he doesn't need nappies. All she ever says is 'Not now, Harry, I'm busy with the baby.' Now I know how my old teddy felt when I sent him to the jumble sale."

On the banks of the stream the willow trees trailed their yellow-green leaves in the water, like girls leaning forward to brush their hair. There were tall plants called policemen's helmets which would have pink flowers, then seed-pods which exploded when you touched them.

Harry settled in his secret den to wait for Kevin.

It didn't look like a den. Three trees grew close together and made a perfect place to hide. Harry kept an old ice-cream box under a root. Inside was half a packet of soggy custard creams and a hat.

It was a fisherman's hat. Harry had found it further along the bank, among the wild forget-me-nots. It was too big, so he

121

had to perch it right on the back of his head to see out, but it was a dull green colour and good camouflage.

Harry's other camouflage was silence. There must only be the churning of the stream on the stones.

In the chocolate-brown mud of the bank opposite there was a hole. Harry stared at it for so long that he saw an odd little face grinning back at him, a cross between a goblin and a water-rat. Harry blinked and shook his head.

There was no face after all.

"Come on, Kevin," said Harry. "I'm cold." The willows met over the water as if they were playing 'Here's the church, here's the steeple' and they kept out the warmth of the sun.

Just when Harry thought he couldn't stay still for one more second, a dazzling blue light darted down the flightpath of the stream like a tiny turquoise Concorde, then hovered by the hole in the bank.

Kevin was here!

Of course, it might have been Kathleen, because there were two kingfishers. Harry had watched them flying at the bank, digging out mud with their bills to make a tunnel.

Kevin disappeared inside.

"Perhaps Kathleen's sitting on the eggs and he's brought her a fish supper," whispered Harry.

Seconds later the kingfisher was back. He paused, then whizzed upstream, swift as a stained-glass arrow.

Harry felt a firebomb of joy explode in his chest. It was river magic! He had his very own secret, his king and queen birds. Kingfishers were rare and rich as jewels.

Back home, he sat on the doorstep to pull off his muddy wellies.

"Hallo, Harry!" said his mother behind him. "Dad's home. He's looking after the baby so why don't we read a book? Or play a game? We never get a chance to do things together now."

"No thank you," said Harry. She would just have to wait.

He ran upstairs and opened his bird

book at the kingfisher page for the ump-teenth time. It said that kingfishers laid six or seven white eggs. They hatched after about three weeks. Then the parents fed the fledglings with small fish and water creatures for another three weeks. They would have to rush in and out, stuffing food into the gaping bills.

"A bit like Mum and her baby," giggled Harry.

The next day at school, Harry drew king-fishers in his Special Topic book. It was difficult to get the colours right, especially the brilliant blue upper parts with the em-erald gloss on the wings and top of the head. Underneath was a chestnut-orange colour like the cinnamon Harry's mum put in apple cake.

Harry wrote about the birds digging out their nest, and then hid his book right at the bottom of his drawer. He didn't want anyone else to see it.

Especially David Snaddlethorpe.

Some children were scared of David Snaddlethorpe. He walked with his arms stuck out and he had a big face with little eyes like currants in a Sally Lunn.

David Snaddlethorpe liked birds, but not in the same way as Harry. David Snaddlethorpe collected birds' eggs like other children collect badges or toy cars.

He's like a great greedy cuckoo, thought Harry. If he ever robbed the kingfishers' nest, I'd want to kill him.

Just before playtime Mrs Green gathered everyone together for news. John Campbell's stick insect had laid lots of eggs, Judith Pottle had been sick all over the new sheepskin covers in her dad's car, and Michael Stenson's little brother had stuck a coffee bean up his nose.

"How's *your* little brother, Harry?" asked Mrs Green.

Harry said, "I've been down to the stream and found a –"

He stopped. All the children were waiting. He saw David Snaddlethorpe's little eyes fixed on him, hard as burned currants.

"I've found an interesting plant," he mumbled. "It's called a policeman's helmet."

David Snaddlethorpe snorted like a pig.

"What a stupid name for a flower," he sneered. "Are the police down there guarding something?"

He looked round to see who thought he was funny. Some children did.

Harry hung his head in shame. He had almost given away his dearest secret, just to show off.

Mrs Green said, "I hope you're careful near the stream, Harry. It's dangerous."

"Mum could hear me scream," he said, thinking, it's the kingfishers who are in danger.

Harry went down to the stream each day on his way home from school. The grass grew long and lush in the spring rain. Harry took an old cycling cape of his dad's to keep in the den. When he put on the cape it was like sitting inside a tepee with your head poking out of the smoke hole.

One afternoon he saw Kevin and Kathleen whizzing in and out with food in their bills and he knew the eggs had hatched.

There would be three more weeks before the fledglings were ready to leave.

At school, Harry worked in his kingfisher book, but at home those weeks were so boring! Mum and Dad only noticed him when he slammed out of the room or when he was pulling his wide-mouthed frog face. The thing that wound them up most of all was his joke eyeballs on springs. Harry loved to frighten his mum with them, turning round suddenly so that the eyeballs bounced out at her. One night she tore them off and shouted, "These will go in the dustbin if you do that to me again!"

So Harry took them to the den. He made a bird-watcher to keep him company. The silly bird-watcher was made from the cycling cape draped over some branches, with the fisherman's hat perched on top. Harry hooked the eyeballs so that they dangled down beneath the hat. He named the bird-watcher Bobby, so that B.B. would watch K.K. with H.H.

Now it looked as if someone had been plastering under Kevin's doorway, because the bank was white with droppings.

Harry's bird book said that the tunnel would be slippery too, and littered with bones and bits of minnow and stickleback. Every time Kevin and Kathleen emerged, they took quick baths in the stream.

That evening Mum said, "Why don't you ask Kevin home to play?"

"He won't be able to come," muttered Harry.

"But you're always on your own," she said.

Rubbish, thought Harry. The kingfishers darted through his mind all the time. He longed for the fledglings to come out into the daylight to learn to fly. That time would be so short. He mustn't miss it. He had a terrible dream. David Snaddlethorpe was waiting for the fledglings too. When they came out, he snatched their little blue bodies out of the air and dashed them down into the mud. Harry woke up trembling.

Harry was beginning to like baby-watching as well as bird-watching. The baby noticed him now and Harry was learning how to look after babies. When Mum went to Parents' Evening, Harry said to his dad, "You'd better get him clean clothes before she gets back. He's covered in banana and she says it stains."

Dad disappeared for clean clothes. Harry knelt down and brushed bits of banana and soggy biscuit off the baby. He whispered, "I've got a friend called Kevin the Blue. He's a kingfisher and he's got babies. You're the only one who knows, Humphrey."

He sang,

> "Kingfisher blue, dilly dilly,
> Kingfisher green,
> No one but you, little brother,
> Knows who I've seen."

Humphrey gave him a big smile. There was one tooth in his pink mouth, like a sharp, peeled almond.

When Mum came home she looked hard at Harry.

She said, "There isn't anyone in your class called Kevin, is there?"

"No," said Harry.

"In fact there isn't a Kevin in the whole school, is there?"

"Don't think so," he muttered.

She wasn't cross. She said, "Your books are beautiful, Harry. I'm proud of you."

Mum wasn't the only one who had looked at Harry's books. When he arrived at school the next morning, he saw that Mrs Green had put his kingfisher book on full display for Parents' Evening. David Snaddlethorpe was peering at it and licking his lips.

"Found a kingfisher's hole, have you, Hodgkin?" he smirked. "I knew there was something up. You've been acting sneaky."

"Don't you dare go near it!" cried Harry.

"Will if I like. It's not yours."

"Yes it is! Well, in a way it is. And anyway, they've hatched so you can't steal the eggs."

"I could have the babies though," whispered David Snaddlethorpe. "I've got a stick like a shepherd's crook and it's good for hooking things, specially things out of nests down tunnels. I could keep some chicks in my old budgie cage now the dog's had the budgie. I could get them stuffed and sell them."

"It's against the law to catch kingfishers!" cried Harry.

David Snaddlethorpe just laughed.

Harry could hardly breathe. What could he do? David would go looking for the kingfishers after school. Harry would have to get there first. He must protect them, even if it meant sitting up all night long.

Harry's eyes hardly left the clock all day. To make things worse, a storm was brewing and he began to get a headache.

Just before hometime Mrs Green sent him to the headteacher to ask for more pastels to finish his kingfisher colouring. The headteacher searched for ages and then said, "Sorry, Harry, we must have used them all up."

When Harry ran into the classroom, only Mrs Green was there. Everyone else had gone home.

He fled without even a goodbye, out into the wind and slanting rain, remembering too late that his anorak was still on its peg.

The sky was dark and full of storm. On the hillside the long grass soaked his legs. He slipped and fell and rolled to the bottom. He lay there panting for breath. What terrible things had Snaddlethorpe done by now? If he had hooked the babies out of the tunnel, they might have fallen in the water and drowned, with poor Kevin and Kathleen fluttering over them, crying in small shrill voices for their children.

"Why didn't I get Mum?" cried Harry.

There was a great splash and an eerie wail.

Harry scrambled to his feet and stared.

David Snaddlethorpe came crashing through the policemen's helmets, setting off a hundred little explosions like bursting pepperpots. He was splattered all over with mud and his eyes stretched wide with terror.

"Bogy man!" he gasped. "Bogy man, lying in wait to get me!"

He staggered past Harry and floundered up the hillside through the long grass. The wind carried his wail, "Bogy man, Bogy man . . ."

132

Harry heard another sound. Flapping.

He hesitated. Then, with his heart beating like a bird trapped against glass, he stalked that sound through the willow trees.

It was coming from his den.

There was a bogy man all right.

It was a bogy bird-watcher called Bobby.

The wind had got inside the cape and blown it out like a balloon and the eyeballs rolled madly.

Harry sank to the ground with relief.

"Thanks for keeping them safe, Bobby," he said.

The storm rolled away and the pale sun swam into the sky.

Harry felt the river magic.

He watched, spellbound.

The little kingfishers came out of the tunnel into the sunlight and clung to the low branches of a willow tree, iridescent as dragonflies.

Then, as if they had been given a secret sign, they burst over the stream in a shower of brilliant blue sparks.

They hovered and returned. Harry tried

to count them, but they flashed away before he could finish.

Kevin and Kathleen hovered above the water, watching and guiding the flying practice.

"It's like a firework display," whispered Harry. "They're even more beautiful than I dreamed."

He decided there were six fledglings just before they finished their display and vanished into the tunnel.

Harry was exhausted, and happy, and hungry too. He set off up the hill for home.

Someone was coming to look for him. It was his mum, with Humphrey clinging to her side like a baby monkey. Harry grinned.

"Come and meet Kevin, Mum!" he said.

The Wind That Wanted its Own Way

ALEX HAMILTON

Nobody likes to wake up before they are ready, and most people are a bit cross when something happens that stops them sleeping when really they should sleep a bit more. That is exactly what happened one morning to Larry, who was very fond of his bed at night-time and did not like to go anywhere near it during the day. Something woke him up when he was not ready for it.

135

As soon as he woke up he felt cross, because he could see straight away that nighttime was almost over, so it seemed silly to try to go to sleep again. But daytime hadn't arrived yet, either, so there wasn't enough light to read a book or paint a picture. Out of the window it was a bit black, a bit white, a bit blue, a bit red, a bit yellow, a bit of everything.

But there was no use in being cross with everybody – because they were all asleep. It wasn't any person that had woken him up, it was only the wind. The wind made this funny noise in the chimney that went *Whooooo-woooo-whooo-oooooooo* and every now and again got more excited and shrill and went *weeeeeeeeee* and that usually ended with something in the garden or the street going *clatterbangcrash*! Larry did not really mind the noise, except he did rather wish he could see what it was the wind had broken.

He thought if he went downstairs he might be able to see better how things got broken when the wind pushed them over, so he jumped out of bed and went to the door. But first of all he told all his animals to stay in bed until he told them they could get up, because he was going to go downstairs and tell the wind to make less noise. Then he tried to open the door.

That was quite hard to do. It was terrifically stuck. But when he had turned the handle, he suddenly gave such a great pull that he sat down, but at least the door was open. And in the same second the wind roared down the corridor and slammed the bathroom door shut with a shivering crash. So Larry ran down the corridor, to see if the door had broken.

It hadn't though. The wood must have been very strong. Just to see if it was really strong, he opened the door and let the wind bang it shut again. The noise was even louder than the first time, but it still didn't break. He did it just once more, to be absolutely certain, and this time a little bit of paint fell off and the key dropped out of the lock. Larry was just walking down the corridor to speak to his animals when an even bigger noise sounded all over the house.

It gave Larry a fright, until he realized it was his daddy's voice from the bedroom, shouting "What on earth is going on out there?" Larry realized his daddy would be cross with the wind for waking him up too, so he thought he would just run in and mention what the wind was doing everywhere, woooo-wooo-wooing down the chimney and squealing about the garden and breaking things in the road – and crashing doors shut. The door to the bedroom where his mummy and daddy slept went the other way, so as soon as he turned the handle it went inside, *thump* against the wall.

His mummy and daddy were sitting up in bed and Larry could see they must be cross with the wind.

"It's the wind," said Larry. "It's a bad wind and I'm very cross with it."

But his mummy said, "Never mind the wind. It's you that's a bad boy running about in the middle of the night and waking everybody up."

"Yes, go back to bed and shut the door," said his daddy, falling back on the pillow so that the whole bed bounced up and down.

It upset Larry to be talked to like that when he hadn't done anything. His eyes filled with tears and he could hardly speak. He said, "I'm not cross with the wind any more. I'm cross with *you*!" And he turned round and went out of the bedroom. It was hard shutting the door again, and that made him even crosser, but he managed it somehow.

He had been going to tell them how the key had fallen out of the lock and that he would put it back, but now he decided he would not do that. Instead, he picked it up and threw it down the lavatory pan. Then he held the door and said, "You are a bad wind, and I am a bad boy, so we are friends. If you like you can shut this door with a big bang." As soon as he let go, the wind did what he asked.

The noise of his daddy shouting had woken all his animals up, and naturally they were also very cross with him for doing it. Larry shouted out to his daddy that he was a very bad man running about in the middle of the night shouting and waking animals up and now he could stay in bed and keep his door shut. And in fact either his daddy had gone to sleep again, or he paid attention to what Larry said, because the door certainly stayed shut. That just made Larry determined to show them what a real bad boy was like.

At that moment the wind made a specially fierce noise down the chimney and all the animals looked a bit scared. So Larry explained that it was all right really, because the wind would be their friend. Some of the animals went on looking a bit scared, sitting there in the bed all round Larry, so he told them he was a bit fed up with that. To make them listen to him properly he punched Teddy on the nose, dropped Rubbish the woollen cat on the floor, sat on Rags the blanket, and banged the heads of the rest together.

Then he gave them all a cuddle to cheer them up. He told them they could come downstairs to meet the wind, but they must promise not to speak because the wind hated to be interrupted. None of the animals said a word, so Larry knew that was all right.

But it turned out he could not take them all down, because there wasn't room to carry them all. So he decided to take Teddy and Rubbish and Rags, who always went everywhere. Then he went downstairs – very slowly because it was still a bit dark.

When he got downstairs he could hear the wind much better. It was a very *pushy* wind. It was going round and round the house trying to get in somewhere. All the doors and windows were shut and the wind sounded furious at not being able to come in. Every now and again it would dash up the garden path and go "flap flap rustle" on the front door.

When it had done that several times Larry put all the animals down and went to open the door. As he was pulling back the bolt he called out, "I'm sorry, wind, that nobody let you in." But when he opened the door he saw it was the newspaper that had been making the flapping sound and the wind just rushed past.

Larry bent down to pick up the newspaper, but as soon as he did, the wind snatched it out of his fingers and threw it in pieces all over the hall. "You really are very bad!" Larry said to the wind. He was rather pleased actually, because sometimes things are not as exciting as everybody says they are going to be, and obviously this was a wind that would stop at nothing if given the chance.

He was just thinking about that, when the wind took the hats off the hat-stand, one after the other, and kicked them all over the place. First Daddy's garden hat, then Daddy's going-to-work hat, then Mummy's rain-hat, then his own sou-'wester. Larry wasn't so pleased about that. "That's *my* hat!" he said sharply, and he put the sou'wester on, so the wind couldn't do anything so unfriendly again. To show he did not really mind about the other hats, though, he kicked a big dent in Daddy's black work-hat.

"Wait a minute," said Larry. "I'm just

going to put the newspaper in Daddy's study." He opened the study door, but the wind didn't wait. It went hurtling right past Larry and spun round and round, heaving papers out of boxes and trays and corners wherever it went, and then sending them sailing around in the air. Some papers went right up to the ceiling and looked as if they were never going to come down. In no time at all the whole room was a terrible mess.

"Gosh, wind," said Larry, "my daddy might be very cross with you, because he's a very tidy person."

But the wind showed no sign of calming down. Larry tried again.

"I'll tell you what, wind," he suggested. "Listen, I think we had better just go and sit down quietly in the front room and I will see if I can find some breakfast."

The wind made a laughing pleased noise, so Larry shut the study door and went across the hall into the kitchen. "Would you like tea or coffee?" asked Larry politely.

The wind could not seem able to make

up its mind, so Larry took down the tea-caddy and the coffee jar and unscrewed the lids to show the wind what was inside. In two seconds the wind had half emptied them both and spread a mixture of tea-leaves and coffee powder all over the kitchen. Wherever Larry looked was turning a sort of brown colour.

"You wouldn't think two little jars could cover the whole kitchen," he said. "You're not only bad, wind, you're very clever as well." Then he showed the wind the inside of the marmalade to see what would happen.

But the wind didn't take any notice of the marmalade. So Larry helped himself to a spoonful. Then he said, "Shall I show you how to throw the marmalade round?" The wind seemed to be waiting and watching, so Larry took the spoon and shot bits of marmalade round the kitchen. It didn't spread as thin as coffee and tea, but it did make interesting shapes where it landed.

The wind made a low whistling noise like people do when they are impressed. It made Larry feel funny looking at the marmalade and coffee and tea-leaves covering the kitchen and he said, "We won't have any more breakfast now. We'll go and sit in the front room with the animals until it gets daylight properly. You can go outside again if you like."

He said "Goodbye" to the wind at the front door and took Teddy and Rubbish and Rags to sit on the armchair by the window in the front room. They all listened to the wind outside and after a time the noise it was making began to make Larry fell a little uncomfortable again. He thought perhaps the wind might be upset because he had not let it stay inside when it looked as if it was going to rain.

Then there was the most tremendous cracking sound, like a bit of wood breaking. He stood up in the armchair and saw that the wind had smashed a branch of the tree where Mummy often tied her washing-line. Next the twigs at the end of the branch began crackling up against the glass of the window-pane.

Although the animals had promised not to speak, Larry could see that they all wanted him to let the wind back in again. He said, "All right, but this is the last room we're going to be bad in. After that the wind will just have to make up its mind to go away, because I don't want to be bad all the time."

Then he undid the catch on the window and the wind dived through with a great howl of glee. It sucked the curtains out, twisted them round and round like a rope and fairly thrashed them against the wet walls outside. They were pink before, with a silver pattern, but soon nobody would ever have known they were pink, and the silver parts had vanished under the dirt.

The broken branch came swinging in through the opening, dropping wet slimy leaves everywhere. Worst of all, it poked a long woody finger out and nicked the heads off a whole row of Mummy's tulips. One vase was overturned and smashed, while the water flowed across the carpet. Like birds landing on a lake, all the cards on the mantelpiece suddenly went floating through the air to join the mess.

Larry jumped down and stood in the

middle of the room with both arms in the air. "I have never seen such a bad wind in all my life!" he cried.

Almost as soon as he had said it, the wind began making less noise. The rain, which had been going sideways in big heavy blobs, now turned into something very fine and soft, falling straight down. The broken branch pulled itself slowly back out of the window and hung sadly down to the ground. The curtains stopped flapping and waving and dancing, and leaned against the window frames as if they were completely tired out.

The wind made a sort of hissing sound, which got quieter and quieter. Larry thought it was saying, "See you some other Saturday," but it was hard to tell exactly, because it was moving further and further away down the street.

It was getting to be real daylight. Larry was a tiny bit cold, so he collected his animals and they all got under the cushions of the armchair. Perhaps they all went to sleep for a while, because the next he knew his mummy and daddy were standing beside the chair speaking to him. They weren't just cross. They were very angry.

"You've torn up the newspaper!" said Mummy.

"You've ruined my hat!" said Daddy.

"It'll take hours to get the kitchen clean and nobody can have tea or coffee this morning," said Mummy.

"I'll have to spend my whole weekend putting my bills in order again," said Daddy.

"You've destroyed these curtains . . ."

"Soaked the carpet . . ."

"My flowers!" said Mummy.

"My apple tree!" said Daddy.

"I've never known anybody be such a bad boy in all my life!" they both said together.

"It was the wind," said Larry. "It wasn't me that was bad, it was the wind. It was a very bad wind. I've never known such a bad wind in all my life."

"It's just as bad helping somebody else be bad, as it is being bad yourself," said Mummy. "And none of this would have happened if you hadn't been helping the wind to be bad."

"And for the rest of the day you can help it be good," said Daddy.

Actually, Larry did quite like helping people be good as well as bad, and in the end he was friends again with everybody. But he did think it was a bit of a cheek for the wind to just go away like that, and let him take all the blame when it was only partly his fault.

That night when they went to bed he said to all his animals, "Next time the wind wakes us up, we'll just go to sleep again, and he can go and be bad in somebody else's house."

The Dress

JOAN GUEST

Like all very plain little girls Margie knew
there lurked inside her a beautiful princess
just waiting to be released. She sat huddled
over her book, shoulders rounded, straight
black hair falling over her eyes, oblivious of
the smallness and meanness of the terrace
house where she lived with her gran and
grandad, sailing in a dream ship over em-
erald oceans, drawn in a golden shell by

white swans to a fairyland, where warmth and joy and happy ever after awaited her ....

"That bairn reads too much," her grandad's rough voice broke through. "Ought to be out playing. Get some colour in 'er cheeks. Come on, Mick," he said to her, using his funny pet name for her. "Get thi' ball, an' we'll have a game in t' street."

Resigned, Margie put down her book, and for ten minutes the old man enjoyed a romp, throwing, catching, chasing while the child with fumbling fingers but nimble thoughts turned the ball to gold, the cobbled street into a gracious court, and transformed the workman's blue overalls into livery of gleaming splendour, until her gran called them in for dinner of mash and sausages.

As she constructed mountains, chasms, rivers and roads in the piled potatoes, making gravy waterfalls, her grandparents planned the afternoon. "Regal? Odeon? St George's?" "It's a musical at t'Tower, an' coloured," said Gran. So it was settled. A bag of Maltesers, a packet of fags and a barley sugar stick from Coxe's and they were off to join the queue for the one and nine's; those, and the warm dark, the plush seats and the flashlights were part of every Saturday afternoon, but today, somehow, was special. As they stumbled into their seats, there *she* was on the screen – riding in a black carriage in a white dress and huge straw hat, and singing with clear high notes, smiling – so beautiful, so perfect. The child was dizzy with admiration and so captivated as the trivially romantic story came to its inevitable ending that she hardly moved a muscle except when the tears of joy and sorrow made long streams down her cheeks and had to be secretly wiped from her chin with the back of her hand.

As they walked home in the gathering dusk, she relived every scene, especially the one where *she* wore that dark-green dress, all down to the floor and glittering with diamonds at the neck, her shoulders all bare, and she just *looked*. Didn't even sing at all.

"Sentimental rubbish!" said Grandad over her head.

"Well, I enjoyed it, and you did as well, didn't you, pet?" said her grandmother. But there was no answer from the little girl. Radiant in that green velvet dress, eyes firmly closed against the reality of Market Street, Margie was whirling round and round a marble ballroom in the arms of a dark-eyed hero, singing like an angel. Just like Deanna on the screen.

A few days later Margie came dashing in from Brownies, her eyes burning with excitement.

"We're having a fancy dress, Gran," she said breathlessly. "We can go as anything, we have to make it ourselves and it's in two weeks and I'm going to make a dress stuck out like an old-fashioned lady, and can I? Please, Gran, please?"

"Now that'll take a bit of doing," said Gran. "Where do you think we're going to find anything like that?" The child's face fell. "Well, I'll see what I can look out, pet. I expect we'll manage something. But you mustn't be too disappointed if . . ." Her voice trailed away for the child had disappeared, rushing off to the book she had put down before she had been forced into her brown tunic and cap two hours before.

The next day as she went to school the child entertained her companions with details of the marvellous dress she was going to wear to the fancy dress party. The picture in her head was so complete that no doubt as to the certainty of having the dress occurred. It already existed – she could feel the softness of the velvet, hear the swish as she walked in it. As the days wore on the rest of the children became just as convinced as she was. But then Gran said that they couldn't really do it. Where was the fine velvet to come from, who was to make such a dress? There was a war on and you couldn't get things, too difficult, coupon, waste . . . the reasons followed one on top of another. But none of it touched the child's mind. There *was* a dress; she knew it. Somehow she was sure she had seen it. She wandered out down the street and into Layerthorpe and over the rubble of Hungate. There were the remains of demolished houses there and you could find treasures like bits of marble for hopscotch, coloured patterned tiles, broken glass glittering like jewels, and flowers and weeds grew over the remains of walls and stone steps. As she sat there in her misery, Margie became aware of Kath. Kath went to Brownies too, but not the same school.

"Wot you goin' as?" she said.

"Not goin'." Margie sulked miserably.

"Why not?"

"Can't get a frock."

"My mam's got 'undreds," said Kath. "We got a shop. An' shoes to match. I'm goin' Japanese with a umbrella like paper."

"Parasol," corrected Margie. Kath sat down.

"You can have a frock off me mam if you like," she said, pulling her hair over her head and tucking the ends into her mouth. "What sort you want?"

Out flowed the description, every detail of it embellished as it grew in the child's mind.

"We got one like that, I think," said Kath. "Green, soft. Ever so smooth."

"Is it tight here?" said Margie, her

155

hands on her flat child's chest and waist. "And long and wide at the bottom, and bare here and here, and no sleeves – well, only a bit – and glittery?" Her voice grew to a squeak with growing hope and excitement.

"Yes," said Kath. "You can 'ave it. I'll ask me mam, anyway," she added with a little caution. "Tell you what. I'll meet you here tomorrow and tell you definite."

Margie ran home elated.

"Nell," said Grandad. "It don't seem right to me. I only hope it's true . . . You know what kids are. Mick, are you listening to me? You mustn't depend on it, now. Her mam might say no. It mightn't fit. Who is 'er, anyway?"

"*Kath*, I told you," said Margie patiently. Of course it would be all right – that was only old Granda'. It always is in the stories, she told herself.

The next afternoon she was already on the sun-warmed stone when Kath arrived.

"OK," she said. "Come on, if yer comin'."

Together they ran over the rubble,

through an alley and down into narrow streets full of old and rather dilapidated houses and shops. One had three balls hanging over the door and Kath stopped. "Here," she said.

The window was a jumble of objects – china dogs, shabby shoes, jewellery pinned on old cardboard, candlesticks, jugs, and a row of old coats, dresses, suits on coathangers filled the back of the window.

"Come on in, then," said Kath, and the doorbell jangled. A thin, tired woman stood behind a high counter.

"Hallo, pet," she said, handing over a parcel. "No good to me. Got it in a job lot. Put in t' shoes as well. Be a bit of fun I expect. You' mam'll have to turn it up a bit. Run along now. Kath's got to get 'er tea."

The parcel was wrapped in newspaper and thin, knotted string. Margie didn't know why but she suddenly felt sick. The shop had a bad smell and was dark. She grabbed the parcel.

"Thank you very much," she said, and ran. She didn't stop until she came to the stone step where she sat down and untied the string with trembling fingers. Out fell the frock – green, satin, unevenly faded to a sickly yellowy white. A few sequins still clung to the deep V-neck and the bias-cut skirt drooped grotesquely. There were frills at the shoulders instead of sleeves, and where she had imagined the wide hooped skirt hung the limp, creased folds. The shoes, dyed to match, had dirty scuffed toes and sequins stuck on the anklestraps. Silently, the child rewrapped the parcel. She searched around the rubble for a slate and began to scratch in the earth where it was softer, slowly at first and then with a mounting panic. Then, when the hole was deep enough, she buried the parcel, covering it over with the loosened earth, and then piling on bricks and stones. She walked slowly back home.

"Well, what happened? Have you got it?" asked Gran.

"No." Unable to face the truth of that green horror of a dress, she lied: "Her mam wouldn't let me have it."

"I knew it!" said Gran angrily, and then

she hugged the child. "Never mind, pet. We'll think of something. Come and eat your tea. It's potted meat from Wright's. You like that, and Auntie Jinny popped in wi' some books for you. They're old, but she got 'em at a sale an' she knows you like to read."

After tea Margie turned for consolation to the books. "Angela Brazil," she read. "Oh, I like these. All about boarding schools and poor girls making good and . . ." She read on as her gran began to clear away the tea-things and then to tidy up the grate. She became absorbed in the story. It was just like a miracle! She could hardly believe her eyes, for in the story the poor companion on the cruise-liner had to go to a fancy dress party and had nothing to wear. As everyone dressed up in expensive costumes she was in despair. And there before Margie lay the answer. It wasn't beautiful but it was easy and the party *was* tomorrow. . .

Gran managed to get everything needed the next day.

"Thank goodness everything's not rationed," she said, as Grandad and she measured and cut and glued. "Now, you just go steady," they told Margie, as they buttoned her into her coat. "Or you'll tear."

She called for Thelma and Mary on the way, and the twins. They were curious and a little contemptuous.

"Where's you' long frock, then? Thought it were green velvet? You always did show off, Margie Woods." But the girl crackled on wordlessly. At Brownies she took off her coat.

"I'm a parcel!" she announced defiantly, in her brown paper, string, sealing-wax, old stamps, tie-on label and all.

"What happened to that dress?" asked Mary, but even to her dearest friend she couldn't admit the truth.

"They said I'd spoil it, larking about," she said, and skipped away to dance around the toadstool.

She won first prize. She knew she would – it happened in the story, and Margie had faith in Literature.

She came forward to Brown Owl who put round her neck a beautiful necklace.

"It's real crystals," she said, "so take

good care of it." The necklace flashed with rainbows much admired by all. But her friends basked in reflected glory as they walked home, each begging for a chance to hold the treasure just a moment to see the colours for themselves.

That night, as she undressed she stood in her vest in front of the dressing-table with the crystals round her neck, pulled the artificial silk bedspread from the bed and draped herself grandly in front of the mirror in a splendid dramatic pose.

"Just like Deanna Durbin in the picture," said Gran as she came into the bedroom. "Now into bed with you."

Acknowledgements

'The Old Man Who Wished He Coulda Cry' by John Agard from *Time for Telling: A Collection of Stories From Around the World* published by Kingfisher Books 1991, copyright © John Agard, 1991, reprinted by kind permission of John Agard c/o Caroline Sheldon Literary Agency; 'Back-to-Front Day' by Paul Biegel from *The Elephant Party* published by Puffin Books 1977, English text copyright © Penguin Books, 1977, reprinted by permission of Penguin Books Ltd; 'Jimmy Takes Vanishing Lessons' by Walter R Brooks from *Haunting Tales* published by Faber & Faber 1973, copyright © Walter R Brooks, 1950, renewed by Dorothy R Brooks, 1978, reprinted by permission of A M Heath & Co Ltd, London and Brandt and Brandt Literary Agents Inc., New York; 'Beauty and the Beast' retold by Michael Foss from *A Treasury of Fairy Tales* published by Michael O'Mara Books Ltd 1986, copyright © Michael Foss, 1986, reprinted by permission of Michael O'Mara Books Ltd; 'The Dress' by Joan Guest from *Thoughtshapes* published by Oxford University Press 1972, copyright © Joan Guest, 1972, reprinted by permission of the author; 'The Wind that Wanted Its Own Way' by Alex Hamilton from

ACKNOWLEDGEMENTS

Bad Boys published by Puffin Books 1972, copyright © Alex Hamilton, 1972, reprinted by permission of the author; 'Small Gorilla and the Parsley' by Anita Hewett from *The Anita Hewett Animal Story Book* published by Bodley Head 1972, copyright © Anita Hewett, 1972, reprinted by permission of Bodley Head, a division of Random House UK; 'A Class Trip' by Margaret Joy from *Tales from Allotment Lane School* published by Faber and Faber 1983, copyright © Margaret Joy, 1983, reprinted by permission of Faber and Faber Ltd; 'The Farmer and the Snake' by Julius Lester from *The Knee High Man and Other Tales* by Julius Lester published by Dial Press and Kestrel Books 1974, copyright © Julius Lester, 1974, reprinted by permission of Penguin Books Ltd; 'The Princess in the Tower Block' by Finbar O'Connor from *The Independent Story of the Year 2* published by Scholastic Children's Books 1994, copyright © Finbar O'Connor, 1994, reprinted by permission of Scholastic Children's Books; 'In the Middle of the Night' by Philippa Pearce from *What the Neighbours Did and other stories* published by Longman Young Books 1972, copyright © Philippa Pearce, 1959, reprinted by permission of Penguin Books Ltd; 'Kevin the Blue' by Caroline Pitcher from *The Independent Story of the Year* published by Scholastic Children's Books 1993, copyright © Caroline Pitcher, 1993, reprinted by permission of Scholastic Children's Books; 'Horrid Henry's Holiday' by Francesca Simon from *Horrid Henry* published by Orion Children's Books 1994, copyright © Francesca Simon, 1994, reprinted by permission of The Orion Publishing Group.

Every effort has been made to trace copyright holders but in a few cases this has proved impossible. The editor

ACKNOWLEDGEMENTS

and publishers apologize for these cases of copyright transgression and would like to hear from any copyright holder not acknowledged.

Knock, Knock

Who's there?

Doughnut!

Doughnut who?

Doughnut open until Christmas!

Why was the cucumber mad?

Because it was in a pickle.

Why did the banana go to the doctor?

Because he wasn't peeling well.

What do you give a sick lemon?

Lemon aid.

What is the difference between a piano and a fish?

You can't tuna fish!

What's worse than finding a **maggot** in your **apple**?

Finding **half** a **maggot** in your **apple**!

What did one **tomato** say to the other tomato?

'You go ahead and I'll ketchup.'

Why did the tomato blush?

Because it saw the salad dressing!

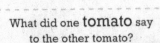